To Marge,
Best Wishes

Jimmy

GUILT TRIP

Written By

James Allen Trick

Dedication

This book would never have been completed if it wasn't for my lovely wife, Dee. The basic story was only half-written when I hit a stall period on writing. At that time, I let my wife read what I had put down on paper to that point, and when she finished she was crying. I knew then I had something going here. A half-written story bringing tears? It needed to be finished.

Dee was my support, my proofreader and critic all rolled into one. She thought it flowed with good anticipation into the next chapter. When I completed a chapter, I turned it over to her for review. I usually watched her as she read it, especially if it involved emotion in the scene. If her eyes welled up while reading, I'd start writing the next chapter because my point was made in that one and her tears proved it. She always told me she couldn't wait to read the next one. Therefore, my first thank you goes to my loving wife.

Next, I need to thank the rest of my family for allowing me to use their names for characters in the book...my three sons, Jeff, Dave and Jeremy, two daughters-in-law, Melissa and Laura, along with four grandsons, Jacob, Cooper, Parker and Brady. It was the first three grandsons which I originally developed into characters in the book, Brady came along much later and I included him at that time. The funny part is that I had the book half-written years before my third grandson, Parker, was even a twinkle in his parent's eyes. It wasn't until after he was born that I realized I picked a character name years before for a character that actually became my grandson years later. Intuition? Who knows? Jeremy and Laura had no idea of the character names in my book when they chose the name Parker for their son. A very strange coincidence, I might say.

I hope this story hits you, the reader, and affects you for a lifetime on some of life's ideals that are presented. No one knows all the answers in life, but just keep an open mind, an open heart and let life run its course.

Thanks again to all my family for their love and support. I love you all.

Preface

Wilderness backpacking is something that has been, and continues to be, enjoyed by people of all ages. The element of being in the wild woods, listening to coyotes, wolves or owls howling through the night along with the element of danger that lurks around every turn of the trail, or every mountain you climb, is absolutely breathtaking and heart pounding. But when you're hiking and camping in the Appalachian Mountains of the eastern United States, where the Civil War was fought from 1861 to 1865, a different sense of awe overtakes you. With all of that history, you never know what, or who, you might bump into. You might even get lucky and be visited at night by a young, Confederate soldier that died in the war back in 1864.

In 1921, former Forest Service employee Benton MacKaye had a radical idea of a hiking trail extending along the Appalachian Mountains. Through much convincing and hard work, sixteen years later in 1937, the Appalachian Trail was completed.

The Trail winds through fourteen states, from Mount Katahdin in Maine to Springer Mountain in Georgia and passes through breathtaking landscapes as the 100 Mile Wilderness in Maine, the Presidential Range in New Hampshire, Shenandoah National Park in Virginia and Great Smoky Mountain National Park in Tennessee. Since its opening in 1937, millions of people have hiked some portion of the Trail, but just over 10,000 have been recorded as hiking the full length.

In 1948, Earl V. Shaffer became the first reported person to walk the entire Trail in a single trip. His 123-day adventure can be relived in his book "Walking with Spring." Earl walked the entire Trail again in 1998 at age eighty.

Hiking the Appalachian Trail, or AT as some call it, can be very rewarding, but also grueling, depending on the shape you're in and how far you want to travel. Elevations vary from flat ground to rises of just under 6,700 feet. Over 350 peaks continue one after another. The actual length of the Trail is uncertain, depending on the literature you read, but the average length at this writing is said to be about 2,175 miles. In 1993, the Trail was walked by three people from end to end with a measuring wheel and put the actual distance at 2,164.9 miles. Modern Geological Survey Maps put the distance at 2,118.3 miles, but that even changes year to year, again, depending on what you read. Any way you look at it, if you travel the entire length of the Appalachian Trail, it would take you about five months and approximately five million steps, give or take a few steps depending on how often you tripped and rolled down a hill.

Also, you must keep in mind the dangers along the way. Remember, you're walking through a wilderness. Besides the normal mosquitoes and black flies that will eat you alive and knaw at your sanity, you need to be aware of rattlesnakes, bobcats, copperheads, coyotes, wild boar, fire ants, rabid skunks and raccoons, elk, moose, poison ivy, poison oak, poison everything, and oh yeah, bears. Don't forget about the bears. And I don't mean the Chicago Bears. I mean black bears. Black bears are plentiful. There are up to an estimated 750,000 of them in North America, many of them in and around the wilderness of the Appalachian Trail, and you better be prepared for anything. They are very unpredictable and usually hungry. Up to ninety-percent of a bear's diet is vegetation, but they will eat meat when it's available. Bear attacks on humans are not very common, they normally run away from you when encountered, but if one is determined to kill you and eat you, it will.

In 1983, a group of people, including a twelve-year-old boy, set up camp along the Trail. They cooked their dinner over the campfire and afterward hung their food in a bag high up in a tree just like books, pamphlets and Rangers tell you to do to prevent animals from getting into it. During the night, a large black bear that, after visiting the camp and climbing the same tree, easily brought down the food bag by breaking the limb where the food was tied. Apparently, the food bag wasn't enough to satisfy him, because he could still smell food in the air. The aroma of the cooked meal had penetrated into the campers' clothing and tents and the 400-pound bear decided he wanted more. He sniffed around until he came to the edge of the twelve-year-old's tent, the aroma of the previously cooked food coming from within, and with one swipe of his claw, the bear split open the side of the tent, grabbed the little boy and dragged him into the woods. Seconds after everyone got out of their own sleeping bags and tents, the boy was dead.

Yes, a morbid piece of information, but you need to be aware that people do die on the Trail. And not just from bears, snake bites or falls off cliffs. Since 1974, there have been at least eleven known deaths from hikers being murdered along the Trail from robberies, rapes or other foul play. Danger lurks everywhere, you need to be on your toes and always be aware of what is around you – including other hikers.

One more fact that people do not realize. Parts of the Appalachians have an annual rainfall that is very close to a tropical rain forest. This can have a great impact on a hiker by considerably cutting down the distance traveled in a day and making parts of the Trail quite treacherous. There can be days when any kind of travel due to bad weather, including heavy fog from the constant dampness in some low areas, is just not going to happen, and hunkering down is the only thing you can do until the weather breaks. When you're used to normally traveling anywhere from eight to twenty miles a day, which is average for an experienced hiker in this terrain, a string of torrential rain days with no travel whatsoever can impact your schedule and distance tremendously, especially if you're supposed to be at a certain point along the Trail on a particular day to meet your ride home. And calling someone on your cell phone to tell them you're running late? Don't bet on it. With the 350 plus peaks that rise over 5,000 feet, the chance of you getting a signal on your cell phone is a crap shoot, unless it's a satellite phone.

Some people go for day hikes, some go for several days or weeks, and still others elect to spend five or six months out of the year to hike it the full distance. Many hike what they can during their vacation time and then go back the next year, continue where they left off and keep returning year after year until they've completed the entire Trail. Many more are just happy to say they hiked the Appalachian Trail, no matter what distance they have accomplished. And most of all, when you hike it, stay on the marked Trail. There are about 165,000 white "blazes" marked on trees, rocks and posts, so you shouldn't have any trouble finding your way. Leaving the marked trail can offer up a nasty time, but following the Trail will bring memories and experiences you will take with you the rest of your life.

Chapter One

Jacob Allen loved hiking and backpacking in different areas of the country. He'd been to various places in Upper and Lower Michigan, his home state, hiked in the Colorado Rockies, the Sierra Nevada and the Yosemite Range, even did some rock climbing and rappelling in West Virginia. But he never hiked the famous Appalachian Trail that runs through the Great Smoky Mountains, Appalachian Mountains and into the White Mountains in the northeast. Actually, West Virginia was the only part of the eastern United States he had been to.

Nearing his fiftieth birthday, he made the decision it was time to hike this part of the country, namely the AT. He didn't plan on traveling the entire 2,175 miles, at least not on this trip, but he knew where he wanted to start and where he wanted to finish. A month long, four or five-hundred miler was plotted out and hopefully he could do this with no problem. Things start to happen as you approach fifty years old; the body reacts differently the older you grow. Aches and pains pop up in muscles you didn't even know you had, and recovery time for injuries take more time to heal. On top of that, your normal hiking pace with a fifty-pound pack on your back seems to slow down also. Instead of walking three or four miles per hour on the trail as you did ten years ago, you now find yourself walking two miles per hour instead. This definitely cuts down your travel distance per day, substantially after thirty days. So, as you grow older you need to take this in consideration and don't plan on setting the same goals you did when you were younger. If you do, you're just setting yourself up for disappointment. In fact, sometimes it's wise not to set any goals at all, just go at your own pace, rest often, take a lot of pictures and stop when you feel it's a good place to make camp. Tomorrow is always another day.

Jacob was a Science teacher at a northern suburban Detroit middle school. He loved to teach his students the fascinations of the Science industry and had an outstanding reputation, especially when performing his experiments. Every Fall when the new school year began and the students received their schedules, anyone who had Jacob for their Science class was excited. They were eager to get to class and see what crazy thing he had planned for the hour. He was appropriately nicknamed "Mr. Wizard" by his students.

School experiments always require extensive planning and thinking before performing in front of a room full of kids. Generally, these experiments were fascinating and went very well, leaving the students' eyes big and their mouths open with excitement. But sometimes for Jacob, they didn't go quite as planned.

One particular time, Jacob had their undivided attention by demonstrating the procedure of how a volcano erupts. Not your simple experiment by using the normal baking soda and vinegar solution, when mixed together makes rapid rising foam, but he decided to use a few different chemicals he found in the Science closet that actually generated a small amount of heat, resulting in a puff of smoke with some rising red goop to simulate lava. He also built a paper-mache, volcano mountain about eighteen-inches tall and painted it the colors of dirt and rock to make it look more realistic. Inside was a hidden reservoir to house the chemicals, with a tube that rose to the top to allow the smoke and fabricated lava to expel, like a real volcano.

With the volcano sitting on the long, black Science table at the front of the classroom and Jacob standing behind, he started adding the chemicals to the hidden reservoir, one at a time, all the while explaining the science behind an eruption and the intensity of the students' faces building by the second.

When he added the final chemical, there was a quick, short puff of smoke out the top of the volcano, which made all the kids jump, then the eruption of red, foamy goop to signify the hot magma followed. The kids were amazed. They all cheered when the volcano erupted. And just like that, the experiment was over. Or so everyone thought – including Mr. Wizard.

Jacob walked around to the front of the table and answered questions from his class, which many students had. About three minutes passed when he saw all of his students' faces at once with a look of horror, pointing at the volcano behind him, because it was beginning to vibrate violently on the table. Jacob turned around just in time to see the top of the volcano blow apart with a huge, mushroom-shaped smoke cloud billowing up to the ceiling. Apparently, the first little puff of smoke was the initial chemical reaction, the only reaction the Science teacher expected. But when too much of the chemicals are sitting in a bowl mixed together for an extended period of time, well, the volcano really erupted.

Instantly, the classroom smoke alarm sounded, triggering the school fire alarm, and then resulting in complete evacuation of the entire school. Six minutes later the Fire Department arrived with three trucks and a Rescue vehicle, but of course, there was no actual fire, just smoke. The Fire Department eventually gave the "All Clear" for teachers and students to return to their classes, after the smoke had been exhausted from the Science room and adjacent hallway. Jacob, however, had some explaining to do to the Principal.

Another time, while teaching his kids about the native tribes and the techniques they used to hunt, he set up a small target on an easel at the side of the room. Jacob had a long piece of hollow bamboo and he was demonstrating how the natives used this similar piece of bamboo as a blowgun, along with darts made of pointed sticks or quills to bring down animals they hunted. The primitive people dipped the tips of the darts in a poison chemical, found in the glands of a tree frog native to their area, inserted the dart into the bamboo and blew hard. The dart became a projectile with incredible speed and stuck into the animal they were hunting. The poison instantly reacted with the animal's nervous system and it dropped over within minutes, completely paralyzed, but not enough to kill it. The natives then approached the animal, slit its throat and had their meal. The poison dissipated while cooking the meat over the fire.

Jacob, however, wasn't using sharp, pointed darts. He knew that might be a little dangerous. He made three darts out of a narrow, wooden dowel, glued a few tiny feathers on them to resemble an arrow and tied a small, lead fishing split-shot, used by fishermen to weigh down their bait on a fishing line, on the end to give it some weight for more distance and accuracy. The target was just a piece of one-inch thick Styrofoam about one-foot square with a bulls-eye drawn on it, resting on the easel. Jacob stepped back away from the target about twenty-feet, loaded the first dart in the bamboo blowgun, raised it to his mouth and blew. The dart flew out with great speed and hit the lower left side of the target, leaving a deep impression to show the hit.

The kids were amazed. They laughed and cheered for Mr. Wizard.

He loaded the second dart. Once again, he raised the tube and blew hard. The dart again shot out and hit the target almost dead center. The students erupted with cheers and applause at how accurate their teacher was with such a primitive weapon. Jacob, feeling quite cocky now, loaded the final dart.

He raised the bamboo one final time and blew with the utmost confidence he was going to hit the target dead center. He did not.

There was a roomful of instant shock when the shattering noise filled the room, then hysterical laughter, with the teacher leading the hysterics. Jacob not only missed the targets' center, he missed the entire target completely. The lead-weighted dart traveled with blistering velocity, right over the top of the target, hit the glass window behind it, obliterating the entire window. That's what the kids loved about him – they never knew what to expect. Once again, Jacob had some explaining to do to the Principal.

Jacob Allen was a single man, been that way for quite some time. But it wasn't always that way. He was married to Annie, the love of his life, whom he had met while attending Michigan State University. They met in their junior year, both getting a degree in teaching. Jacob loved Science and Annie was into Biology. They were a good fit.

After graduation, they both were awarded teaching jobs at different schools in the Detroit area, but they were only about thirty-miles apart, so dating continued on a regular basis.

Annie was a very attractive woman. She stood five-feet-eight inches tall, had long auburn colored hair down to the middle of her back and when she started her teaching career, she looked younger than her twenty-four years. Even after six years of college, she still looked like a high school student, which is where she was teaching Biology. Her students, the boys of course, always had a crush on her. She was the kind of teacher that every man wished he had in high school so he could say, "Man, you should've seen the hot teacher I had for Biology."

Annie and Jacob dated for two more years before they were married. Both being teachers and having the three summer months off together, they hiked and backpacked in all kinds of places. He loved the Science they found on these trips, and she loved the Biology. They constantly gathered information, samples, photos and anything they could find useful to bring back and turn it into a learning lesson for their students. This is why everyone loved their teaching…it just wasn't textbook all the time.

One trip they took was out in the Arizona desert to see what they could find, Jacob wanting different pieces of rock formations and Annie trying to study plant and animal life. While hiking in different areas, not far from each other, Annie came across a tarantula that made a burrow in the sand. She found this quite fascinating and wanted this creature in her classroom. Gathering coarse dirt and sticks and putting them in a two-quart container with a snap lid, she snatched up the spider and enclosed him inside his new temporary home, poking small air holes in the lid. She then tucked him away in her backpack. If Jacob ever found out she had a tarantula with her to bring home, he would absolutely freak out. He did not like spiders of any kind. If he saw a spider on the wall at home, he'd scotch-tape it to the wall, sit and stare at it to make sure it didn't get away and wait for Annie to get home to remove it. She knew she couldn't say a word about the tarantula.

On their drive back to Michigan from Arizona, Annie checked on the container periodically in her backpack when they stopped for gas just to make sure the six-inch long little guy was doing okay. She did this only when Jacob went inside to pay for the gas, so he couldn't see what she was doing.

They got back home late at night and decided to unpack the car in the morning. After driving twelve hours that day, they were exhausted and just wanted their own bed. When morning came, they both unpacked the gear, the samples of rock Jacob retrieved on the trip and various items Annie had picked up along the way. Afterward, Jacob said, "I'll be back in fifteen-minutes. I'm going to go get a car wash," and away he drove.

Annie went inside and started unpacking her backpack when…oh shit! The container's open! Sand is everywhere! There's no tarantula! He's got to be in here somewhere! She always left the pack zipper open a few inches to keep air around the container. But unfortunately, there was no spider anywhere to be found.

Jacob pulled up to the drive-thru car wash and said to the attendant, "Give me the works. I've got a lot of things to flush out of this one."

He paid for the deluxe wash, pulled forward and set his shifter into neutral. A moment later, the car was being pulled into the carwash and the soap started spraying. The jets fired high-pressure water and the vehicle looked like it was driving through a hurricane. The vibrations, the noise, the fresh smell of soap, Jacob knew his car was being cleaned to the max.

Then, suddenly, something appeared to the left corner of his eyes. Movement. Not outside the car. Inside.

On top of the dashboard, in the left corner, was a vent with large openings for the defroster. Reaching out of this vent were a couple of long, hairy legs. A quick jump forward and the tarantula was sitting on the dash in front of Jacob's face and making his move toward him. Jacob didn't even have time to get out a scream before he flung open the car door and dove out into the deluge of water. Yes, the car was only halfway through the carwash, but that didn't matter to him. The only thing that mattered was that there was a spider the size of a dinosaur on his dashboard and he needed to get out…NOW!

The carwash shut down instantly and attendants

came running from both ends to see why Jacob was running and screaming like a little school girl to get as far away from his car as possible. When they finally got him calm enough to speak, he said, while covered in soap and water, "There's a huge, furry, crawly thingy in my car!"

One attendant went over to look inside the car, now soaked throughout because the door was open, and searched all over, but found nothing. When he came back with a blank look on his face, Jacob insisted something was still there, saying, "I am not leaving until you find that thing", and he made them all go look again. Just then, one of the attendants found the dead, drowned tarantula lying under the vehicle in a pool of water. When he showed Jacob what he'd found, all Jacob could do was yell, "DAMMIT ANNIE!" Now Annie had some explaining to do.

They were married six years before their son, Jimmy, was born. Jacob, being the only surviving male to carry on the family name, was ecstatic. His grandfather had one son, Jacob's dad, Herm, and his dad had one son, Jacob. It was up to him to keep the family name alive. And it was alive again, with Jimmy.

After Jimmy was born, Annie decided to take a

leave from teaching for the next three years to be a stay-at-home mom and teach their son the values of family life that they loved and cherished. Jacob couldn't wait until Jimmy was old enough to start playing baseball. He even took Jimmy to a Detroit Tigers baseball game when he was two, but that only lasted three innings before Jimmy decided it was time to go. A two-year-old only sits still for maybe…never. That was okay though; the Red Sox pounded the Tigers that day twelve to two.

At age three, their little boy was already smarter than most kids his age. Annie taught him how to count to twenty and say his ABC's. He'd even walk through the garden with her, picking up worms, toads and an occasional Praying Mantis and played gently with them, only to return them to their habitat when he finished. He was taught to never harm the wildlife. Jacob, however, would cringe whenever Jimmy held his hands up in front of his nose and said, "Daddy, look what's in my hands!"

There was a time they had a serious scare when Jimmy came down with pneumonia. He wasn't getting any better and the fever rose to a hundred-and-four. They eventually had to admit him into the hospital where he stayed for weeks getting treatment. At one point, the doctors weren't even sure if Jimmy was going to make it through the night and Jacob saw his whole world crumble around him during that time. For two weeks, his students wondered what happened to Mr. Wizard, because he wasn't his cheerful self and wouldn't do his crazy experiments for them. His job was teaching the kids, but his mind was obviously somewhere else. Jimmy finally came home three weeks later and Mr. Wizard was right back at it again with his crazy experiments.

Jacob grew up with sports and never got enough of it. He once said if he ever got divorced, he would marry sports. That's how much he loved it. So, you can see why he couldn't wait to get Jimmy involved in baseball, football, hockey, basketball, you name it. If it had anything to do with sports, he wanted him into it.

When Jimmy turned six, it started. Tee Ball. Jacob played baseball with Jimmy for a year before Tee Ball started, so playing this so-called Tee Ball game was much too easy for Jimmy. He got easily frustrated with the other kids because they didn't play as well and he didn't know why. He just knew they were all lousy compared to him and it made him mad.

Throughout the next few years, Jimmy turned into a great ball player. At age nine, he was the star pitcher of his team and batters already feared him. He threw such a powerful fastball that some of the batters bailed out of the batter's box when they saw the ball leave Jimmy's hand. Nine years old, already intimidating on the mound. And Jacob was eating it up.

Annie and Jacob had many "discussions" about Jimmy's performance as a ball player. Annie thought Jacob pushed too hard to get Jimmy where he was, she thought he shouldn't be taught about the pressure of winning all the time and that he should just play for the fun of it. Jacob always apologized and agreed with Annie - until the next game.

By ten, Jimmy was tossing a wicked curve ball that got him pulled out of a few games. Not because he didn't have control and was dangerous to the batters, he had complete control, but the opposing parents put up such a gripe that something had to be done. The batters, their kids, never had a chance to hit the ball. The local newspaper even did an article on "Mr. Wizard's Wizzer", as he became known. He was someone that nobody had seen pitching that well in ages. The crowds grew larger when Jimmy pitched;

everyone wanted to see this Wiz Kid. During one game, he pitched to twenty batters - struck out sixteen of them. But, unfortunately, it wasn't a no-hitter; the very first batter he faced backed out of the box from fear when the ball was coming and the fastball clipped the bat for a clumsy bunt. The batter took off and was safe at first base for a lucky hit. Jimmy was a phenomenon in the making and the entire town, statewide news media and even ESPN knew it.

With Jimmy involved in so much summer baseball, Jacob and Annie found it difficult to plan any family vacation time. Most games were played one night during the week with the second game played on Saturdays. Occasionally, the Saturday game was waived and replaced with another weekday game. Those particular weekends that were free were the ones they all went camping together. They usually stayed locally in Michigan, not spending more than a few hours driving time to get where they wanted to go. Sometimes it was a State Park Campground, other times it was driving down a two-track road into the northern woods and finding the ideal camp spot next to a river or small lake. That was everyone's favorite -

away from the crowd and just roughing it. They were tent campers, no pop-up campers or motor homes for them. Just a large tent, sleeping bags and a small shovel to bury your...well, you know. And of course, the things you need for camping, including a camp stove, fishing poles and lanterns.

Their favorite place to go was just a three-hour drive north of Detroit, in the eastern part of the Northern Lower Michigan wilderness. Jacob parked at a trailhead off the main highway, loaded everyone with their backpacks and then they hiked the three-mile trail through the woods to the far side of a small, remote lake.

One July weekend, there were no baseball games scheduled, so Jacob decided it was a good time to hit the woods. They left early Friday morning and after three-hours, they arrived at the trailhead of their favorite spot. Jacob pulled out their backpacks and they started their three-mile trek through the woods to the secluded lake. Along the way, they passed a small pond named Carp Lake. Carp Lake was only about four acres in size and was nestled in a low depression to their left. The trail skirted along the ridge and followed the lake on two sides before heading deeper into the woods. Jimmy heard some splashing noises and noticed some activity on the lake. Sound travels so much easier and is noticed a lot better in the woods when there are no sounds of traffic or people nearby. He asked, "Hey dad, can we go down to the lake and see what's going on? I hear splashing."

"Sure," said Jacob. "We have no schedule in the woods."

Jimmy led the way as Jacob and Annie followed their little explorer. It was about a hundred-yards downhill to the water's edge, meandering through trees, bushes and ferns. Finally, reaching the lake's shoreline, Jimmy yelled excitedly, "Beavers!"

There were two beavers swimming on top of the water, one was swimming across to the opposite side of the lake gathering twigs and branches with lots of leaves and then bringing them back, the other beaver was dragging larger branches, almost logs, back across to their den. It looked like one was gathering food and the other was doing home repair and maintenance. The splashing noise was from their tails - every time they dove under the water, they'd smack their flat tails on the water, making a loud splat. Jimmy was amazed by their activity and they sat and watched them for about an hour before heading back up the hill and down the trail.

They arrived at the west side of the larger lake about mid-afternoon and found nobody around but themselves.

"Hey Jimmy," Jacob said. "Keep following the trail to the east side of the lake. There's a great camping spot there with a sandy beach."

"Okey dokey, daddy-o," he said.

All of a sudden, Annie froze.

"Guys, don't move," she said quietly. Jacob thought that maybe she saw a bear or something. He grabbed Jimmy's arm and held tightly, slowly moving him behind him in case the bear attacked.

Annie cautiously reached in her front pack, pulling out what Jacob thought was bear pepper spray. She raised it to her face and then he heard, "Click, click." It was her camera.

"What the heck are you doing?" Jacob whispered. "A camera is not going to stop a bear, unless he's camera shy."

"A bear?" she chuckled. "You idiot. It's an owl."

Apparently, it's rare to see owls in the middle of the day with them being nocturnal animals and hunting at night, so this was a real treat for her. As they slowly walked by, the owl never took his eyes off them, following every move they made until out of sight. Annie was so excited, because this was her first owl sighting in the wild. She hoped to see much more wildlife over the next couple of days, while Jacob hoped not to see any bears.

Jimmy went on up ahead and minutes later yelled, "Mom, dad, over here! I found the spot!"

Up over the next hill brought them to him. He was standing on a flat area of ground, tall trees behind him and sandy beach and lake in front.

"This is where we camp. I love this spot," he exclaimed. "We have all the woods and trails behind us, a sandy beach for swimming and the lake for fishing. This is what I want."

"Okay boss," Jacob said. "Let's make camp."

Annie had her clothes, food and camera equipment in her backpack. Jimmy carried mainly his clothes and fishing gear. Jacob had his clothes, tent, camp stove and lanterns. Each of them had their own sleeping bag strapped on the outside of the backpack.

While Jacob set up the tent, Annie and Jimmy gathered firewood for the campfire. There was plenty of downed wood on the ground and things were really dry this time of year. They built up a good stockpile of kindling and larger branches while Jacob finished setting up the tent. When completed, he gathered logs and cut them into small pieces with his collapsible saw. The huge pile of wood would only last one night so they needed to do this every day they were there.

"Hey Jimmy," Jacob said. "See if you can find some large rocks so we can make a fire pit." He wanted to make sure they contained the campfire in one area. They surely did not want the fire to get a chance to spread with all this forest around.

"Okay, dad," he replied. Jimmy wandered along the lakeshore and then up the hill behind their camp. A few minutes later, he called out, "Hey mom," because she was the animal expert, "looks like someone brought their dogs here. There's dog tracks everywhere back here."

Annie went up to have a look.

"Well, you're almost right. They look like dog tracks," she said. "They're actually coyote tracks. Looks like there's a pack of coyotes in these woods. Don't wander off too far alone, coyotes are unpredictable."

"What will they do?" he asked.

"Just don't wander off, okay?" she said sternly.

"Okay mom," he said.

It was getting to be early evening when Jacob said to Jimmy, "Hey Mr. Fisherman, feeling lucky?"

"Luckier than you," he said in that cocky way.

"Well then, grab your pole, Lucky Dog," Jacob said. "Let's see if we can catch some dinner."

Annie perched herself on a nearby log with a book while the boys walked down to the water's edge. They dug up some worms and baited the hooks, then tossed their lines out into the calm water. The sun was starting to set over the trees on the far side of the lake and the bugs were flying low over the water, signaling dinnertime for the fish. Soon, the fish were jumping out of the water grabbing their gourmet meals.

Jacob's line jiggled a few times then stopped altogether. A few more minutes passed with no activity when he said, "I'll bet they took my bait."

Jacob reeled his line in and sure enough, a bare hook was the only thing on his line.

"Do you need me to show you how to bait a hook?" Jimmy asked with a smirk.

"Mind your own business, rookie," he said.

Jimmy laughed. Jacob baited the hook and tossed his line back in the water. Just then, Jimmy's line went tight and the pole bent down. Then it shot left, and then right. The pole nearly jerked out of Jimmy's hands.

"Whoa, hold tight Jimmy!" Jacob yelled. "Start reeling him in!"

Jimmy reeled slowly, but the fish fought hard. Back and forth, up and down, that fish was pissed. Finally, Jimmy got him close enough to the surface to see what he was. It was a three-foot northern pike. To Jimmy, it looked like a whale. Jacob stood by and coached him on what to do to get that fish landed, and after twenty grueling minutes, the fish was on the shore. Jimmy was exhausted, Jacob was a proud daddy and Annie was screaming at how big the fish was.

"Looks like we have dinner," Jimmy said.

"Yes, we sure have dinner. I hope you're hungry."

Jacob escorted Jimmy and his catch about twenty-yards off into the woods.

"Dad, where are we going?" Jimmy asked.

"We're going to clean the fish. We need to get

away from camp because the fish smell might attract wild animals during the night, and we don't want wild animals near our camp," Jacob said.

"You mean like coyotes?" he asked.

"I mean like anything that lives in the woods," said Jacob.

Jacob dug a long, deep hole in the ground, and then found a flat piece of log to lay the fish on while gutting it. He then laid the flat log in the hole with the fish on it and sliced open the belly. The fish guts dumped into the hole and when they finished gutting and cleaning it, they buried the remains to prevent the smell from permeating the night air.

Annie got the campfire going while the men were prepping the fish, so by the time they came back, the fire was ready to cook on. Jacob cut the fish into shorter sections, seasoned it with salt and pepper, wrapped it in tin foil and placed it on the hot coals. The fish slow-cooked for forty-five minutes and then it was dinnertime.

By now, the woods turned dark with night and campfire light and lanterns illuminated this part of the forest. Jacob, Annie and Jimmy had a great wilderness feast of fresh fish and wild rice that Annie cooked on the camp stove.

Full bellies made all of them drowsy and they sat around the fire listening to the sounds of the night woods. An occasional hoot from an owl, chatter from a raccoon or jumping fish and croaking frogs kept them from dozing off completely. They soon realized it was time to call it a night and crawl into their nylon wilderness condominium.

About 2am, barking and howling dogs, not far away, awakened Jacob.

"Do you hear that?" Jacob asked Annie. "What the hell are dogs doing way out here?"

"Coyotes," she said. "A pack of them, probably less than a hundred-yards away. I bet they found your fish guts."

"But we were careful to bury everything in a deep hole," Jacob said.

"Doesn't matter. If they're hungry they'll sniff out just about anything."

"Are we in any danger?" he asked.

"No," she said. "They don't want anything to do with us. Just be careful when you go out and pee, they might bite something off."

"Very funny, very funny," he said. "You'd be out of luck if they bit that off."

"Shush. Jimmy might hear you," said Annie.

"Great. Now I need to hold it all night. I'll be damned if I'm going out there to pee now."

At 5am, there was an ear-piercing screeching, whistling noise right above their heads that literally scared the piss out of Jacob. Yes, he peed his pants.

"What in the hell was that?" he yelled jumping up.

"Relax. It was a screech owl. Probably in the big tree above us." Jimmy woke up and they both looked at Jacob and burst out laughing.

"What happened to you? Your pants are all wet," Annie said laughing.

"I peed my pants, okay?" he said. "That stupid owl scared the piss out of me. Why? Because I had to hold it all night, that's why!"

Jimmy looked at Annie and said jokingly, "Mom, I didn't know dad still wet his bed."

Jacob, frustrated, said to them, "This does not leave this tent. If anyone finds out about this, I will have to kill both of you." They all laughed until their sides hurt.

It was times like this that Jacob realized how much he loved his family. They were a real close and loving group, loved doing things together and cherished the times they shared. Jacob was blessed to have such a perfect wife and son. He thanked God every day for his blessings.

It was a Friday night in late August and summer baseball had just ended days before. Annie and Jimmy were out at the grocery store and then stopping for ice cream on the way home. Jacob was home working in his study getting things together for the new school year starting in one week. They asked him to come along so he could get his favorite dessert, a hot fudge sundae sprinkled with crushed peanuts and a cherry, but he had so much to do that he decided to let Annie and Jimmy have some alone time together for a change. They were disappointed, but it was really okay, because during baseball season, it seems to be all Jacob and Jimmy.

At 7:40pm, the phone rang. Jacob didn't want to be bothered because he was so busy preparing, but he answered anyway.

"Mr. Allen?" the voice on the other side said.

"Yes, this is Jacob Allen. May I help you?"

"Mr. Allen, this is Lt. Moross from the Police Department. There's a medical emergency and you need to come to the hospital right away."

Jacob's heart was in his throat.

"What do you mean, a medical emergency?" he said.

"It's your wife and son, sir. You need to come down to the hospital immediately."

"Oh God, are they okay? Is anyone hurt? What can you tell me?"

"Mr. Allen, please, come to the emergency room right away."

Jacob knew this was not good. Not offering any kind of positive news from a medical emergency means not good. He left his house crying before he was out the door. He knew something terrible had happened, he could feel it.

It took fourteen-minutes to get to the hospital. Jacob ran inside the ER entrance yelling, "Annie, Jimmy, somebody please, where's my family!"

An officer met Jacob at the counter and said, "Mr. Allen? Come with me."

He took Jacob into a private room; Annie and Jimmy were not there.

"Where's my family? Please! Where's my family!"

"Sir, I'm sorry. There's no easy way to say this. There was this…drunk driver. He ran the red light doing over 60 mph and broadsided your wife's car. Your wife…and son…they…died at the scene. I'm very, very sorry sir."

Jacob wasn't sure what he just heard. It couldn't be what he thought.

"Wha…what? What did you say?"

"I'm sorry sir, your wife and son…they…didn't make it. They're gone."

The entire world just stopped. The love of his life, his cherished wife, his only son, the future star of Major League Baseball, gone. Just like that. Gone. Because of one idiot driver that chose to get behind the wheel of a vehicle when he was clearly not capable. Wrong decision. Wrong driving. Everything wrong, wrong, wrong. And now - Jacob was alone.

He sat with his head in his hands for hours, insisting this had to be a bad dream and he was going to wake up in bed any minute, next to Annie. But the bad dream was a true life-changing nightmare. He didn't wake up in bed, he finally opened his eyes…he was still at the hospital.

Jacob couldn't help but think if he had gone with them, as they asked him to, maybe something would be different. It's possible they wouldn't have reached that intersection until a minute later and not even come across the drunk driver. He thought, "If I had said yes instead of no, we could all be at home right now, together. Oh my God, this was my fault. This was my fault. I should've gone with them. "

Reality finally clutched his heart and squeezed so hard he thought he was going to have a heart attack. He broke down, sobbed…, sobbed…, and sobbed. He felt he was the reason they're dead. His guilt told him he should have gone with them. It wasn't actually his fault, but nobody was going to convince him otherwise. How could he possibly go on with his life? His life was his family. His family was his life. Now he had no family, therefore to him no life. Sure, he had the new students at the about-to-begin school year to occupy his daytime and keep him busy. But what about when he had to return home to an empty house? Annie's things would still be hanging in the closet; her smell would still linger in the bedroom. Her hairbrush would still be sitting on the dresser with strands of her auburn hair tangled within the bristles. Her boxes of shoes remained in their closet.

And what about Jimmy? Pictures of Jimmy were scattered everywhere throughout the house. You couldn't turn in any direction, in any room, and not see Jimmy somewhere. In the garage was Jimmy's bike, his sled, his roller blades and various remote control toys; out in the back yard was the little tree house the two of them built together last summer. Even Jimmy's baseball bat and glove were still standing in the corner of his room, waiting for Jimmy to pick them up again and play.

But playing ball again wasn't going to happen. Watching Jimmy fly into the big leagues wasn't going to happen. Seeing him graduate, go to college, get married, have children - not going to happen.

Sharing ideas for experiments and watching Annie's excitement or laughter, not going to happen. Taking those cherished hiking trips together as a family and learning so much more together, not going to happen. Even contemplating the idea of having a second child together and growing old with each other, becoming grandparents, retiring one day and living a beautiful life until the end of days - sorry, not happening. The end of days was here, right now, in this room, for Jacob.

Chapter Two

It took Jacob quite a while to prepare for this trip to the Appalachian Trail. For one thing, he started a rigorous exercise program for four months before leaving. After his family's death eight years ago, he let himself go because of depression and gained thirty pounds during the first two years. After that, he tapered off and remained the same weight until his recent training program. He was by no means grossly overweight, but he wanted to be in much better shape if he was hiking the Trail.

He had not gone hiking or backpacking once since Annie and Jimmy left his life. Jacob spent the eight summers being somewhat of a hermit; he did not leave the house unless he had to, shied away from any time with friends, never traveled or ever left town. Nothing was the same anymore. He had no desire to do much of anything. During class time, he was the infamous Mr. Wizard to the students, because he felt no matter how hard his personal life was, he could not deprive those kids of anything less than an exciting education. So, wild experiments continued with laughter and learning, at least as much as he could get himself to do.

But when he returned home, it was like being Dr. Jekyll and Mr. Hyde. Dr. Jekyll was the fun-loving science teacher everyone knew, and Mr. Hyde was the private, depressed man nobody knew. It just had to be that way.

This was the summer that Jacob decided he must finally get on with his life. Going backpacking would help to rejuvenate him and give him a wonderful time to think, remember and heal while being in the wilderness, away from people and the busy life. He was privately depressed for eight, long years; something had to change and it was up to him to change it.

He climbed up into the garage attic and pulled down all of his hiking and camping gear. Backpack, small camp stove, mummy sleeping bag and inflatable mattress, camp pillow, foldable wood saw, water bottles, water filter and pump, one man tent, fireproof matches, Swiss army knife, multi-tool, flashlights, various ropes, cords and bungees, candle lantern, compact gas lantern, binoculars, rain gear, hiking boots, walking stick, camera, that's just to start. Then, he had to pack clothes, all kinds of clothes because you never know what kind of weather you're going to be subjected to, buy extra boot laces, freeze dried food, snacks, instant coffee, bug repellant, sunscreen, first aid supplies, biodegradable soap, toothpaste, batteries, candles for the candle lantern, camp fuel for the stove and lantern, and whatever else he could think of. All this going in one pack, strapped on his back.

The first-time Jacob decided to try backpacking, in the days before he met Annie, he just went out to a local store, bought whatever he thought looked good and seemed affordable. He knew nothing about the extremely lightweight backpacking gear that was available; he just bought what seemed good to him. Therefore, needless to say, his first five-day solo trip was terribly exhausting, because he carried a pack on his back that weighed nearly ninety pounds. He could barely lift it up to strap it on. Ninety pounds. That's like carrying a small person on your back for ten miles a day, five days in a row.

That only happened once. After that trip, he

decided to get some advice from a salesperson in the backpacking store on what to buy. His new pack, with all new gear, including tent, sleeping bag, smaller stove, all new equipment replacing everything he previously bought that was excessively heavy for hiking, fully loaded with clothing and food, weighed less than fifty pounds. Quite a difference. And very manageable for long trips.

When the school year ended, Jacob got all his gear together and left Detroit, riding on a travel bus to a town called Harpers Ferry at the northern tip of the West Virginia-Maryland border. This is where he wanted to pick up the Appalachian Trail and start his trek. From there, he planned to hike the AT southwest through Virginia, into North Carolina and Tennessee, until he reached his planned destination at Great Smoky Mountain National Park. The month-long hike covered approximately four to five-hundred miles and meandered through many areas where the Civil War battled from 1861 to 1865. Who knows, if he was lucky, he might find a relic or two along the way to take back to class. When completing the trip, he planned on grabbing another travel bus and heading home.

After a very long bus ride, he arrived at the bus stop in Harpers Ferry at nine p.m. Jacob then walked to a local motel and secured a room for the night. His wilderness journey would start in the early morning hours after a good night's rest and a hearty breakfast at the local pancake house.

The next morning, he headed for the Trail in town where it crossed the footbridge on the south side of the Potomac River. Harpers Ferry is nestled on a point of land between high, rocky bluffs where the Potomac and Shenandoah Rivers meet. Thomas Jefferson once described it as "perhaps one of the most stupendous scenes in nature". At this point, you can see West Virginia, Maryland and Virginia all at the same time. This town is where Stonewall Jackson set up his headquarters for a time during the Civil War.

Harpers Ferry is home to the Appalachian Trail Conference Headquarters, also known as the ATC. Since 1972, the ATC staff has educated hikers about the Trail's history and what to expect when traveling the footpath. They also offer volunteer programs for maintaining and restoring the trail itself.

When the AT winds upward out of Harpers Ferry

and across the Shenandoah River Bridge, it passes by Snickers Gap and Ashby Gap before entering the northern tip of Shenandoah National Park in Virginia. This is a breathtaking stretch of real estate when the weather is clear, however most panoramic views are now obstructed by heavy growth. The first eighteen-mile section from Harpers Ferry south is the original section of trail, blazed by the Potomac Appalachian Trail Club in 1927. When you are standing on top of the ridge, you can easily see why Harpers Ferry changed hands so many times during the Civil War - it was virtually a sitting duck at the confluence of two major rivers and well below the high bluffs above. Basically, it could be attacked by land or rivers, and it certainly was, many times over.

Many Trail areas are nicknamed "The Green Tunnel", because the trees overhang the Trail, thus creating the tunnel effect, letting little sunlight penetrate through the leafed branches. There is also a thirteen-mile section that hikers call "The Roller Coaster", because it traverses ten mountain peaks, ascending and descending each peak until you are completely exhausted.

Shenandoah National Park is one-hundred-and-one miles long and serious hikers can cover the entire park in about five days, hiking roughly twenty miles a day. It has a very large whitetail deer population and the most black bears of anywhere along the 2,175 mile Trail. That averages out to be more than one black bear per square mile. So, if you're going to encounter a bear, Shenandoah Park is probably where it will happen.

Eventually the AT exit's the Park at Rockfish Gap. From there the AT parallels the Blue Ridge Parkway and crosses it several times. Along the way, it visits places like Salt Log Gap, Tar Jacket Ridge, Hog Camp Gap, Johns Hollow, Punchbowl Mountain and Matts Creek before it crosses Interstate 81 near Cloverdale, then heads west for Lost Spectacles Gap, Sinking Creek, Dismal Branch, Dragons Tooth and Lick Skillet Hollow. It then bends around Pearisburg, heads back southeast along a ridge system known as Brushy Mountain, until it reaches the Grayson Highlands, Mt. Rogers and Whitetop Mountain, before descending to Damascus, commonly known as one of the friendliest towns along the Trail. But in reality, most of the towns the Trail passes through are very hiker-friendly. At this point, Tennessee is about three miles southwest of Damascus and the Trail heads for the high country there, climbing into Iron Mountain, the Roan Mountain Massif, Unaka Mountain and Beauty Spot. At Erwin, the AT crosses the Nolichucky River, climbs No Business Knob and travels along Bald Mountain, Hogback Ridge, Frozen Knob and many other wonderfully named ridges. Once at Hot Springs, North Carolina, the Trail crosses the French Broad River before ascending Max Patch and the Snow Bird Mountains.

Finally, after crossing Pigeon River, the Appalachian Trail enters Great Smoky Mountains National Park for about seventy miles, with much of the Trail above six-thousand feet. Somewhere along this stretch is where Jacob planned to end his journey. A long, demanding, exhausting thirty-day, four to five-hundred-mile walk. He was finally on his way, starting at Harpers Ferry, West Virginia.

Jacob hiked through town until he came across the Appalachian Trail Conference Headquarters. He checked in with the personnel at the counter and described his planned trip to them. Melissa, a college student helping for the summer, took Jacob outside on the covered porch and said, "Now stand right there while I take your picture for the log book," and snapped a Polaroid photo of him. Minutes later, after the photo was developed, Jacob filled in the required information under the photo with his name, address, emergency contact information, how far he planned to travel and duration of travel time. The completed photo slipped into a clear notebook jacket and inserted in the registry album, along with all the other AT hikers. This way, they could keep track of him in case there was an emergency.

"You know," Jacob said, "there really is nobody to contact if I'm in some kind of emergency trouble. The only name I put down was my boss."

"That's okay," Melissa replied. "We seldom have to use that information anyway, but we need to show something with your photo."

Melissa directed him where to pick up the Trail and after he did, the Trail immediately crossed over the Shenandoah River Bridge to the other side of the river. Jacob was now walking on the Virginia-West Virginia border. The AT immediately ascended six-hundred feet to the top of the ridge.

This section of trail, from the bridge to Snickers Gap, is a fairly, easy walk along the ridgeline. It's mostly remote, even though Jacob passed by a number of developed areas he could see below the ridge. Nearly twenty miles into the hike, Jacob came across the Potomac Appalachian Trail Club's Blackburn Trail Center, which marks the beginning of a part of the Blue Ridge that becomes more rugged and soon enters Shenandoah National Park at Front Royal.

As he passed by Snickers Gap, the Trail started to wind back and forth between the hollows and gullies; this is the area that the PATC declared to be more strenuous and tiring than any section in northern Virginia.

Jacob felt good when he crossed into Shenandoah National Park; he had been walking for nearly thirty miles already today. Since the hike to this point had been fairly flat and easy, he made good time. It was nearly six p.m. when he hit the more challenging part of the Trail and continued on his journey.

The Blue Ridge really becomes the Blue Ridge in Shenandoah Park. The Trail ascends to over four-thousand feet and the park is nearly two-hundred-thousand acres, so traveling away from developed areas is not much of a problem. This is where Jacob finally started to feel his excitement grow. Hiking in the wilderness, away from civilization and people - except for other hikers, and enjoying the serenity of the forests and animals and stars and waterfalls and streams - how could this be any better?

The Blue Ridge area in Shenandoah Park played a big role during the Civil War. The hills and bluffs provided shelter for both the Union and Confederate armies, and rocky outcrops were perfect perches for lookouts. Numerous battles took place in and around this stretch of the Blue Ridge, countless men and young boys died from both sides. All of them were fighting for something they believed in - it turned into a brother against brother war for four, long years.

At eight p.m., Jacob decided he better find a place to make camp for the night. There are trail shelters built along the way, but he didn't know when he was going to happen upon one, so he found a nice area off the Trail to pitch his tent and settle down for the evening.

It didn't take long to erect his wilderness home, maybe ten minutes, and afterward, he decided to make something to eat before retiring for the night. The night sky was clear, dusk was approaching rapidly and some stars were becoming visible. Jacob dug out his small camp stove, placed a pot full of water on it to boil and stretched out his sleeping bag in the tent. A few minutes later, he had boiling water for his freeze-dried chicken and rice dinner with enough water left to make a large cup of tea.

After dining, he cleaned his utensils, put the trash in a zip-lock bag and threw a rope high over a tree branch. He then tied his food bag on the end of the rope and hoisted it up about twelve feet to keep the critters from getting at it, namely the bears. Then he hooked his backpack on a broken branch about five feet off the ground.

Jacob leaned against a log and gazed into the dark, clear sky for about an hour before he turned in for the night. The weather looked promising for tomorrow to continue the journey into Shenandoah.

The battle at New Market in the Civil War took place on May 15, 1864. New Market was a small, Virginia town in the Shenandoah Valley where Union Lieutenant General Ulysses S. Grant thought he could press the Confederate Army of General Robert E. Lee into submission and end the war. Grant ordered Major General Franz Sigel to move his men up the

Shenandoah Valley to destroy the railroad and canal complex at Lynchburg, while Lee had Major General John C. Breckinridge advance his troops to New Market. At the time of battle, the Union came with 6,275 soldiers and the Confederates numbered 4,090. The Confederates also had 257 cadets standing by from the Virginia Military Institute (VMI) ready for battle, but none of these young men had ever seen fighting. The original plan was to not send in these cadets, unless absolutely necessary. The boys ages ranged from fifteen to twenty-one, but most were seventeen and eighteen.

In a drenching rain, the Union artillery let loose a relentless barrage of cannon fire and the Confederates soon realized they were in deep trouble. Major General John C. Breckinridge of the Confederate Army said, "Put the boys in…and may God forgive me for the order."

The boys began their descent down Shirley's Hill at a walking pace because nobody told them any different, but when they realized they were being fired upon, they broke into a fast run. At the bottom of the hill, they were ordered to discard all unnecessary gear and charge forward with rifles and swords in hand while the Union Artillery was reloading. The boys never faltered, they charged across the rain soaked Bushong Wheat Field with the mud being so thick, it sucked the shoes off most of the cadets. For this reason, the field was later named "Field of Lost Shoes." The charge continued and Sigel's defense collapsed. Now threatened by the Confederate cavalry on his left flank and rear, Sigel ordered a general withdrawal, burning the North Fork Bridge behind him. Grant was very upset with Sigel's performance and soon replaced him with Major General David Hunter.

Five cadets died at the battle scene, five more died later from injuries and forty-seven were wounded. Overall, the Confederate casualties numbered five-hundred-and-forty and the Union casualties totaled eight-hundred-and-forty. The battle today is still viewed as an example of youthful heroism.

A rustling awakened Jacob outside of his tent. He checked his watch - it was 3:40a.m. The noise was somewhere close to his backpack and food bag hanging in the tree. He listened intently, heart pounding harder as the rustling continued. All he could think of was a bear. He knew bears were plentiful along the

Blue Ridge, could he have encountered one on the first night out? The noise it was making did not sound like it was large enough for a bear, but it sure sounded bigger than a raccoon or possum. He dared not to unzip his tent door or window, for fear of drawing attention to himself, so he just laid there and continued to listen. After a few more minutes, the disturbance ceased and was gone.

The bright morning sun made its debut on Jacob's tent at five-thirty. He awoke to the warmth of a beam of sunshine beading down where his head was resting against the side of the tent. Suddenly, he remembered the noise last night and he unzipped his door to see if anything was disturbed. He panned the area with his eyes and saw nothing looked out of place. Jacob crawled out of the tent and walked over to his backpack, still hooked on the tree, hoping to find some kind of animal tracks in the soft dirt around the area.

There was nothing. Not a single print other than his own boots. He thought that was a little strange, knowing he definitely heard something out there. Could it have been some kind of animal just tree hopping, found the backpack and then moved on when it couldn't get into it? The food bag was undisturbed also.

Whatever is was, it didn't leave tracks or rip anything apart.

Jacob packed up his sleeping bag and tent and made a good, quick breakfast of oatmeal, granola bar and coffee before he hit the Trail. The day was beautiful, the air smelled fresh and woody and he started his day two hike about seven-thirty a.m.

Chapter Three

A half-mile down the Trail, Jacob came across one of the shelters. It had three sides enclosed with planked wood, a screened front with a door, wood floor and metal shed-type roof.

"Great. Why couldn't I have come across this last night," he said. "So close and yet so far, as they say."

The Trail then ascended quickly to the ridge at Compton Gap, about 2,400 feet, and stayed close to the ridgeline for a while. He soon came upon a family of hikers, a man, his wife and son. Jacob couldn't help but stare at them as they approached from a side trail down the hill. They reminded him so much of Annie and Jimmy. He could see himself walking with his family on the Trail as this family was doing.

"A great morning to you, fellow hiker," the man

said.

Jacob smiled and replied, "And a good morning to you and your family also. Is that a different trail you just came up from? I don't see the regular trail markings there."

"Yeah, it's a beautiful side trail leading down to New Market," he said.

"New Market?" Jacob asked. "Is that some kind of farmer's market or something?"

"No, it's a little town that had a nasty battle during the Civil War," he said. "Kinda like a mini-Gettysburg."

"Well, that sounds like it would be worth the trip, but I think I'm staying on the main Trail. Trying to get to the Smoky Mountains in a month," Jacob said.

"Wow, you've got your work cut out for you, my friend."

Jacob looked at the man's wife and son and said, "You've got a great family. It's nice to see you all doing something together," he said softly, "Reminds me of my family."

"You look like you're traveling alone. I'll bet your family misses you very much," the man said in a very kind manner.

Jacob's eyes started to well up and he replied quietly, "I don't think as much as I miss them." He bid farewell and walked on down the Trail.

The Trail shortly began to traverse from peak to valley and knob to gap. Walking the easy ridgeline was now a thing of the past. It went from 3,400 feet at Hogback Mountain to 2,400 feet at Elkwallow Gap in just three miles. Then it went back up to 3,500 feet at Mary's Rock. Mary's Rock is a great boulder pile, overlooking Thornton Gap. Francis Thornton, who claimed the area and built a house here in 1733, named the rock after his wife. Jacob was rapidly becoming exhausted and knew today's hike wouldn't cover nearly as much ground as the previous day. The day remained fairly clear, but by mid-afternoon, the clouds started rolling in and it appeared he might be in for some wet weather soon.

Jacob came across the Big Blue Trail, often called Big Blue, a side trail that leads to many waterfalls within the park. He decided this would be a worthwhile detour, possibly coming across some interesting things near the waterfalls.

About three more miles down the Trail, he came to Big Falls. At ninety-three feet, it's the tallest cascade in the park. He wandered around the large pool made by the pounding water from above looking for artifacts, but found nothing of interest. Before long, the weather began looking dismal and Jacob happened upon a shelter where he decided to pack it in for the night. The shelter was small, only two wood bunks inside, with a table between the two. The walls were wood planks, no windows, except for the front, which had screened frames above the three-foot high wall and a door in the center. The floor was also wood planked, covered with many small holes in the corners, with evidence of mice living beneath and making their way onto the main floor. Jacob was sure he'd have tiny visitors tonight.

The rain began shortly after he stretched out his sleeping bag and set up a few things inside, roughly eight o'clock. It started out with a drizzle, then became a steady shower. By the time Jacob had dinner and was ready to call it a night, a full-blown thunderstorm had arrived and dropped torrential rain all over the Blue Ridge.

Heavy rain continued for hours, thunder clapping near and far in wave after wave. It wasn't until midnight that Jacob finally fell asleep. At least the shelter kept him warm and dry.

The rain ceased briefly and the pitter-patter of many, tiny feet inside the shelter awakened him around one-thirty a.m. He couldn't stand not to look. Jacob grabbed the flashlight next to his sleeping bag and turned it on. Suddenly, mice scattered everywhere. There must have been over fifty of the little creatures. On the table, on the floor, up the walls, even on the bunks. Almost all of them immediately tucked back into the cracks and holes to get beneath the floor, except a few brave souls that remained curious. Jacob yelled and threw his socks at them and they ran for cover, but he knew they would return later when things quieted down. The rain continued into the night and Jacob fell back asleep to the rhythm of the raindrops.

Once again, he was awakened to footsteps, but these were not of mice. He thought he heard someone walking on the front porch of the shelter. Though he looked through the screens from his sleeping bag, he could not see anyone. Jacob looked at his watch - it was once again 3:40a.m., just like the previous night.

"That's weird," he thought to himself.

Maybe, another hiker finally came across a shelter through all this rain and needed a place for the night.

"Hello? Is anyone there?" he shouted.

The footsteps stopped.

"I've got room in here if you need to get out of the rain," he said.

He heard nothing.

Jacob unzipped his sleeping bag to go look. He heard the footsteps leave the porch.

He opened the door and saw what appeared to be someone quickly disappear into the nearby trees. The rain and mist made the figure look ghostly, almost transparent.

"I know you must be soaked," Jacob said. "Come on in here, where it's dry. No need to stay out all night."

Jacob stood in the doorway a few minutes, but saw or heard nothing more. He couldn't figure out why someone would prefer the rain over shelter. Only two things came to mind - either the hiker preferred solitude with nobody to have to talk to, or that person was there to rob him of his gear. He shut the door and tied the handle with a bootlace. Even though the entire front of the shelter was only screen and someone could easily cut it open if they wanted to, the tied door still gave him a small sense of security. Jacob went back to bed and after hearing no more noise, soon fell back asleep.

"RIGHT ACROSS MY FACE!" Jacob screamed. "A MOUSE RAN RIGHT ACROSS MY FACE!" He jumped out of his sleeping bag and the mice were everywhere. It was almost daybreak, the rain ceased and he figured he wasn't going back to sleep now. The mice hid instantly when Jacob lit the candle lantern and the shelter lit up with light. He pulled his sleeping bag off the bunk and shook it out. Two more mice dropped out of the bag and scampered away. All Jacob could do was chuckle.

By the time he finished cooking and eating breakfast, the morning sun broke through and started warming the damp air. Jacob walked outside to look for the footprints in the mud from last night's hiker - again there were no prints anywhere. He walked over to the spot where he saw the figure walk into the trees, a very muddy area, there was nothing. No prints of any kind.

"I don't get it," Jacob thought. "Unless they got washed away from the rain. But you'd think there'd be something, somewhere." He packed up his gear and was once again back on the Trail moving south.

The Trail was quite muddy and slippery in many

places from last night's rain and Jacob slipped and sloshed along the way. Occasionally, he came across other hikers, but he was surprised at how few there were. Summer is a big time for travel, especially on the AT, and he could only attribute the scarce people due to the isolated area he was traveling in right now. He knew farther down the Trail there would be many more hikers as he neared local towns and villages, so he savored these alone moments and used them to clear his mind and collect his thoughts about his life.

He thought often about Annie and Jimmy; he knew they would've loved it here. Thinking about them brought him back to near depression, but he tried to stay focused on making this his recovery trip and getting his life back. It was okay to think about them, even reminisce about the good memories, but it was time to move forward. They would always be in his heart, no matter what direction his life took him.

Before long, Jacob arrived at Stony Man Mountain. At 4,011 feet, it's the second highest point in Shenandoah Park. At the southernmost end of the mountain is Skyland, a resort area that has shops and a campground for those who prefer somewhat modern camping as opposed to roughing it in the wilderness. Jacob ventured into one of the stores there to stock up on a few needed items, snacks and refill his water bottles.

The woman behind the counter was perfect for that job. She had a bubbly personality, looked deeply into your eyes when you spoke to her, and was very attractive. She was probably in her late thirties, tall and slender, wavy shoulder length brown hair and beautiful, hazel eyes that sparkled and smiled even when she wasn't smiling herself. The extremely revealing low-cut blouse helped in selling more goods, I'm sure. Jacob couldn't help but stare at her beauty when he went to the counter to pay for his items.

"Hi sugar," she said with a slight southern drawl as he approached. She also gave him a look up and down as if she was checking him out. "Something I can do for you?"

"Hello," he replied. "I'm just grabbing a few things while I'm here."

She gave him another up and down look, this time with a smile.

"Grabbing a few things, huh? I like a man that grabs what he wants," she said winking.

Jacob looked up. He couldn't help but smile. "I'm...uh...hiking the Trail."

She leaned forward over the counter to get as close to him as possible, her blouse falling open and offering a tremendous view of her busty cleavage.

"Well, since you've been walking for awhile, maybe you could use a shower and someone to wash your back?"

Jacob, mesmerized by her little show she was putting on, was just about to say something in return when a man walked in from the back room. He had a full, black beard, red plaid shirt, like a lumberjack and was over six-feet tall and well built.

"I see you've met my wife," the man said while walking by the counter.

"Uh, yes, yes I have," Jacob said nervously. "She was just checking me out. I mean, not checking *me* out, but...you know, checking out...what I ...have. I mean the...stuff. You know?"

The man looked at Jacob as if he was some kind of weirdo. In the meantime, the woman put his items in a bag and said, "That's twelve-fifty-five, darlin'."

He paid her and left nervously without saying a word. He just wanted to get out of there as quickly as possible. When he got outside, he checked the bag to make sure everything he grabbed was there. While looking at the receipt to double check the amount, he noticed on the back it said, "I close at 9pm. Shower? Nancy."

Jacob immediately crumbled up the receipt, threw it in the garbage can and hurried away, hoping her husband had no idea of what just happened, but he couldn't help but smile when he left.

Back on the Trail and just east of Skyland, Jacob could see Old Rag Mountain in the distance, separated from the main ridge by a deep, narrow gorge. It's reported to be the most spectacular peak in the Central Appalachians, resembling the Goat Rocks of the Cascades in the State of Washington, but on a smaller scale. This great mountain, with its nearby waterfalls and shattered rim rock, attracts thousands of hikers every year. It houses the first "Byrd's Nest" shelter, a series of shelters designed and financed by former Senator Harry F. Byrd, Jr.

A couple of miles down the Trail brought Jacob to Hawksbill, the highest point in the Park at 4,051 feet. Jacob took a loop trail to the summit between the AT and Skyline Drive, the highway that runs the length of Shenandoah National Park and turns into the Blue Ridge Parkway farther south. The summit was covered with red spruce trees, the species found at high elevations as in Smoky Mountain National Park. Three hikers, all young men maybe in their thirties, approached from the opposite direction and stopped to talk with Jacob for a few minutes before moving on.

"Afternoon," one said as he came close.

"Good afternoon, fellas," Jacob replied.

They stopped and dropped their packs to rest for a bit. Jacob did the same. "Are you guys hiking far on the Trail?" Jacob asked.

"We've been at it all day, had a little rain down by Milam Gap, but it wasn't enough to stop us," the tall one said.

The blond-haired gentleman asked, "Are there any General Stores or anything just north of here? We need to get some supplies."

"As a matter of fact, there's one about five miles up in Skyland," Jacob said. "They've got anything you need, and more…believe me. Even showers. Just ask for Nancy."

"Hey, thanks man," they said. "Can't wait to get

there."

"Watch out for the lumberjack," Jacob said jokingly.

"What? A lumberjack?"

"You'll see," said Jacob. "Just be careful. It's a small area and some people get bored. They love to see new faces and are looking for something to do."

All three looked at him with a puzzling look on their face. They hoisted up their packs and headed north, while Jacob continued to head south.

Chapter Four

One of the cadet casualties at the Battle of New Market in 1864 was Thomas Garland Jefferson, the grandson of Thomas Jefferson. He died three days after the battle. Some died within days, others weeks later. All of the 257 cadets charged the Union line valiantly that rainy day, without fear or even knowing they were badly outnumbered. Even though none of those young boys ever saw battle before that time, they obeyed their orders without question or disrespect to their commanding officer and marched forward. The bravery of those boys turned a defeat into victory for the South, pushing the North into retreat and keeping control of the Shenandoah Valley to the Confederates.

Jacob only had a couple of daylight hours left, so he started looking for a place to camp for the night.

A shelter would be ideal, due to the fact that dark clouds were getting close, probably the rain the three hikers came across near Milam Gap. He knew he was near Tanners Ridge Overlook because of the signs earlier on the Trail. Just rounding the next turn, he spotted a shelter. Once again, as the night before, this was a two bunk shelter with a table in between, and it was empty.

Jacob set up his gear inside and went out to look around the area. To the east were the headwaters of Rapidan River; this river flows between Fork Mountain and Doubletop Mountain. A side trail that runs along the river takes you to Rapidan Camp, favorite fishing retreat of former President Herbert Hoover. The President used to fish from the front porch because it was literally right on the river. Back then, Shenandoah Park was just in the process of being developed.

To the west was a beautiful overlook of Tanners Ridge. The ridge, at 3,465 feet, ran pretty much north and south and Jacob could see the sun setting over the ridge top. He gathered some firewood while walking back to the shelter to have a nice fire for the evening. The mountains of the Blue Ridge, though not comparable in height to the Rocky Mountains, can experience some extreme drastic weather changes. The Rockies tower at over 14,000 feet, while the Blue Ridge and Appalachians barely rise above 6,000 feet. But even a few thousand feet in altitude change can create some interesting weather. Although in the high Rockies it can snow furiously at any time in late summer, the Appalachians might be having a nice summer shower in the valley while torrential downpours and suddenly dropping temperatures can endanger hikers with the threat of hypothermia on the peaks. This concerned Jacob as weather started moving in, because he wasn't in the valley, he was on the ridge.

Darkness settled over the Appalachians as Jacob's campfire vigorously crackled through the silence of the spruce trees. After a quick dinner, he sat back and pondered thoughts about Annie and Jimmy until he dozed off next to the fire, now only glowing embers.

A low rumble off in the distance awakened him. Another rumble, a little closer, got his attention. A bright flash suddenly made him aware the storm was approaching. The wind picked up, noticeably chillier on top of the ridge, and a loud crack of thunder forced

Jacob into the shelter. He lit his candle lantern and checked the time; it was nearly 10:30pm.

The shelter appeared as if it had some recent repairs. A new-screened front, new roof boards and new front porch were obvious. He knew with new roof boards, there must have been a new roof also, so he planned on being totally dry all night. The storm continued to build outside, but he knew he was safe inside. Jacob crawled into his sleeping bag and hunkered down for a long night of steady rain, the sound relaxing him and dropping him into a deep sleep.

He woke a few times and upon hearing the rain and thunder continuing through the night, turned back over, and fell back asleep. He was right - he was staying dry and protected from the nasty weather outside, and so were the mice. He knew they wouldn't really hurt anything and just accepted them as his night guests. But the first one that came across his face, he'd be having mouse stew the next day.

The temperature dropped during the night into the low forties, a dismal cold on a wet night. Jacob climbed out of his sleeping bag shaking, so he opened his backpack to find another sweatshirt to put on to keep warm. Something caught his eye.

Out at the campfire site he saw someone kneeling, stirring around the ashes to spark the fire again. Jacob didn't say a word, he just watched through the front screen. Thinking it must have been nearly daybreak, he looked at his watch to check the time. It was 3:40am - again.

This was really starting to bother Jacob. Three nights in a row, waking at 3:40am, he couldn't help but think there was something strange here. He watched in silence as the stranger continued to stir the fire. As lightning flashed, Jacob could see that the man appeared to be wearing what looked like a gray, short, wool coat, dirty gray pants and a cap of some kind, not really a baseball cap, but close. After another bright flash, Jacob was able to see a little of his face. It wasn't a man after all, it was a boy, a teenager maybe. But something looked funny. He wasn't real clear; sharp body outlines could not be seen. Jacob figured the rain and humidity created a misty look between him and the boy and that's why he had a foggy look about him.

Jacob sidestepped in the shelter to get a better look and bumped into the stool at the table. The boy suddenly looked up at him just as a bright flash of lightning blinded Jacob's vision. The thunder immediately clapped and when his vision cleared, the boy was gone.

He went outside with a flashlight and looked around the campfire pit. It was still raining quite hard, but he could see where the boy rustled the ashes and coals in the pit. Something else got his attention. There were no footprints in the mud. He knew the rain could not have washed them away so quickly and this really puzzled him. Three nights in a row, waking at 3:40am, never finding any footprints, people fading into nowhere - something's going on here.

Jacob couldn't sleep the rest of the night. He sat at the table in the dark, staring out at the campfire site, hoping to see the boy come back sometime.

He didn't.

Daylight broke with light rain still coming down and Jacob made some tea and hot oatmeal for breakfast. Still puzzled about last night's event and the previous night's events, he had a difficult time processing all the information. No matter how many times he tried to put things together, he just kept coming up with nothing. Over and over he'd ask himself, "Why at 3:40am? Who is this kid? Why is he here and what has it got to do with me, if anything? And why no footprints?"

Eventually he got things packed up, left the shelter, dissatisfied, and confused.

Chapter Five

Hiking was muddy and sloppy from all the rain with the drizzle continuing into the late morning hours. The ceiling, as weather people call the thick layer of clouds, was extremely low. That meant the top of the ridge was smothered in cloud cover and fog and Jacob was walking with limited vision, only being able to see about ten-yards ahead of him. No other hikers were present on this part of the Trail as he approached the summit of Hazeltop, some 3,800 feet high. Dismal weather can keep people bundled in their tents or shelters until the weather breaks, so Jacob figured that was the reason for no passersby. Why slop around in the rain and mud when you can be warm and dry in your shelter? If he had known how miserable it was on the Trail, he would never have left his dry hut at all. Too late for that kind of thinking now.

By early afternoon, the drizzle had turned into a steady rain again and traveling on the Trail became quite treacherous. A few times, Jacob traversed the Trail alongside rock ledges that dropped a hundred-feet or more off to the side. Mud and loose rocks made it challenging, even deadly if not careful. Jacob tripped on a jagged rock in the path and went down face first into the mud, sliding downhill and catching himself before he slid too close to the edge. Another couple of feet could have been disastrous.

As he approached Bear Fence Mountain, he saw a shelter. The weather wasn't letting up at all and he heard thunder off in the distance, big thunder. Although it was only around 3pm, he decided he better stop for the day and hold up in the shelter for the night. As he approached, he heard voices coming from within.

"Hello, anybody there?" Jacob yelled.

Just then, two people came to the screen door and looked out.

"Uh, hold on a second there buddy," the man said.

Jacob heard a lot of rustling and giggling coming from inside and knew it must have been a guy and his girlfriend enjoying the seclusion together, surely not expecting anyone to come and interrupt them.

A minute later, the screen door opened, an embarrassed couple standing there saying, "Okay, come on in out of that rain."

"I'm sorry," Jacob said. "I didn't mean to interrupt anything."

"Aw, that's okay," he said. "My name's Joe. This is my girl, Carolyn."

"Hello Joe, Carolyn. I'm Jacob. I was kind of hoping nobody was here so I could bunk down for the night."

"You still can," said Joe. "We're staying another night because of the weather, but we're only using one bunk, you know what I mean?" he said winking. "You can feel free to use the other if you like."

Jacob, a little apprehensive at spending the night with a couple of co-eds, heard the thunder getting closer and said, "Well, are you sure you don't mind?"

"Of course not. We're all friends on the Trail. As long as you're not an axe murderer or something," Joe said laughing.

"JOE!" Carolyn yelled. "I can't believe you just said that. That was mean."

Jacob chuckled and said, "Don't worry. I haven't chopped anybody up in over a week."

The look of sober shock on their faces was precious. Jacob could see the gears going around in their heads wondering what they just got themselves into. Seconds later, when they realized it was a joke, they all burst out laughing.

"Take that bunk over there Jacob," Joe said. "Well, I guess you could've figured that out yourself."

As Jacob dropped his pack and started unpacking his sleeping bag and a few dry clothes, he asked, "So, where are you guys from?"

"Fayetteville, West Virginia," Carolyn said. "We drove to Front Royal at the north end of Shenandoah Park and left our car there, then took a bus to the south end at Rockfish Gap, where we started. We're hiking the full Shenandoah Park Trail."

"That's a decent hike, hundred-miles," Jacob said.

"A hundred-and-one," Joe replied smiling. "But who's counting?"

"Should take you about five days or so. Well, I guess that depends on how long you two stay in the shelters," Jacob said laughing.

"Yeah, might take us all summer!" Joe smirked. Carolyn nudged him aggressively in his ribs. "And how about you? Where are you from?"

"Detroit," said Jacob. "I started at Harper's Ferry and am going down to Smoky Mountain National Park."

"Wow", they both said simultaneously. "That'll take you...hell, that'll take you a really long, fucking time!"

"Not really. Only about a month if I maintain a steady pace."

"Hiking alone, that's tricky. You have to be really careful you don't sprain an ankle or something," Joe said.

"I know. I almost lost it about a mile back on a loose edge," said Jacob. "The drop-off would've killed me for sure."

Joe looked Jacob up and down a little and said, "Detroit, huh? Pretty rough there, isn't it?"

"Well I'm still here, so...that must mean it's not really rough or I'm one bad-ass guy!" Jacob replied with a stern voice.

Joe looked him up and down again and said, "I think it's not really that rough." They had a good laugh.

The young couple started cooking their dinner on a camp stove on the table inside the shelter when Jacob said, "You know, you really shouldn't do that in here. You should cook outside on the porch. This park has the largest population of black bears of anywhere in the country. That food smell could draw them in tonight."

"I've never had any trouble before, why should I expect it now?" Joe said smartly.

"I just don't think it's a good idea tempting fate," Jacob said cautiously.

Joe and Carolyn continued cooking and feasting afterward, the smell of spaghetti and meatballs lingering throughout the shelter. Jacob elected to cook his dinner outside on the porch. The shelter overhang protected him from the rain while the thunder clapped loudly.

A couple of hours later, the rain finally ceased and Jacob could see the couple packing up their gear and getting ready to leave.

"What are you doing?" Jacob asked. "You're not leaving, are you?"

"Yeah, we are", Joe said. "Carolyn says she's not comfortable with what you said earlier about bears.

Thanks a lot."

"I didn't say it to chase you guys out," said Jacob. "I really think you should stay the night."

"Sorry man. We're outta here," Joe said sternly. "Watch out for those so-called bears you're so worried about." And they were out the door.

Great, Jacob thought. Now I'm the one in here with all the food smell. I should've been the one to leave.

The more Jacob thought about it, the more it bothered him to stay in the shelter all night. He decided to pitch his tent nearby and sleep in that. He wasn't in the mood for a large, carnivorous visitor to pop in and tear him apart, looking for food. The tent was probably the safest bet, but by the time he got it all set up, the return of the pouring rain had drenched the tent inside and out. He was forced to use the shelter after all.

Jacob awakened during the night to some loud noises outside the shelter. He looked at his watch - it was 3:36am. At least it wasn't 3:40am again, he thought. Something was walking on the shelter porch, just outside the door. Jacob strained to see through the darkness, but couldn't make out who was there.

"Hello?" he said. "Do you need shelter for the night?"

A growl.

Jacob's heart raced and was in his throat. A black bear, surely drawn in from the smell of cooked food coming from inside the hut, was sniffing around on the porch. The door starting jiggling from the bear pushing on it with his nose. Without any further effort, the screen door came crashing to the floor inside. Jacob froze while peeking over the edge of his sleeping bag. He could see the big, black meat eater lumber through the doorway into the shelter. The bear's nose was high in the air, sniffing while moving his huge head side to side. He stared straight at Jacob, knowing there was something in that sleeping bag he wanted. It seemed like eternity passed while Jacob watched the bear staring at him, and then the bear took a step towards him.

Suddenly, a loud bang occurred on the front porch; the bear turned and ran out the door, frightened by the noise. Jacob yelled, "Who's there?"

No answer. He looked at his watch - 3:40am.

Jacob got out of his sleeping bag and walked over to where the door used to be hanging. As he was looking outside for the bear, he saw the distorted figure of a man, just across the clearing, about twenty-yards away. The man was just standing there, looking at Jacob.

"Thanks, friend," Jacob yelled. "I thought I was a goner."

The man continued to stand there. The rain had ceased but there was a misty fog hanging in the air. Jacob couldn't make out a clear picture of the man. He then asked, "Do you want to come in the shelter for the night? I've got plenty of room, but unfortunately no door."

The figure stood mute, then started to walk slowly toward him. Jacob was a little apprehensive at what might take place, something seemed very odd. The man came closer. As he approached, his figure in the mist became somewhat clearer. He was a young man, teenager probably, dressed in a gray, wool coat and gray pants. His clothing looked like some kind of uniform, like a boy would wear if he was in a military school or something. The boy was wet, muddy and appeared to be confused. He was now standing ten-feet in front of Jacob.

"Son, are you okay?" Jacob asked. "Come

inside…please."

Jacob turned and picked up the broken screen door, set it aside, and walked into the shelter. The young man slowly followed.

"Please, sit," Jacob said softly.

The boy sat down, looking at Jacob, looking around the shelter, not saying a word.

"Thanks for scaring that bear away, I thought for sure I was dead," said Jacob. "You don't seem to have any supplies. Are you camping nearby?"

The boy looked confused, his eyes still looking around the shelter.

"My name's Jacob, what's yours?" Jacob asked.

The young man stared at him and said, "Thomas, sir."

"It's a pleasure, Thomas," said Jacob. "And you don't have to call me sir. Can I get you something? Coffee? Tea? Something to eat?"

"I don't know where I am, sir," Thomas said.

"Are you lost? How long have you been out here?" Jacob asked. "Your name is Thomas…Thomas what?"

"Thomas Garland Jefferson, sir," he said. "But people usually just call us Johnny Reb."

"That's an interesting name," Jacob said. "Are you named after the former President, Thomas Jefferson? Are you a descendant of the family?"

"Yes," the boy said. "I'm his grandson."

"Grandson?" Jacob laughed. "I don't think so. Jefferson was President in the early 1800's. That can hardly make you his grandson over two-hundred years later. More like great, great grandson."

Thomas looked at him and said sternly, "President Thomas Jefferson was my father's father! Why are you calling me a liar...sir?"

"Calm down, calm down. You can't be his grandson because that would make you...over a hundred-and-fifty years old!" Jacob exclaimed.

"What are you talking about?" Thomas cried. "We're at war here, Major General Breckinridge gave the cadet charge and you're making jokes? Sir?"

"What?" Jacob asked with a puzzling look. "War? Breckinridge? What cadet charge?"

"Sir, the war we've been fighting for three years! The Confederate Army will prevail!" Thomas exclaimed.

Jacob looked at him shockingly. Confused, and trying to muster some words, he finally said, "Son, just who the heck are you?"

"I told you, Thomas Garland Jefferson, Virginia Military Institute Cadet of the Confederate Army, sir!"

Wait a minute. Clearly, this is a joke of some kind. A boy dressed in a cadet uniform, people calling him Johnny Reb - the nickname used to describe a Confederate soldier, says he's the grandson of Thomas Jefferson, fighting a war? Jacob was getting really confused here.

"What war did you say you're fighting?" Jacob asked.

"The War between the States, sir," Thomas said. "You're not a Yankee, are you?"

"Son, that war ended in 1865", Jacob said. "Are you doing a reenactment around here?"

"1865?" Thomas asked surprisingly. "This is 1864, sir."

Now, more confused than ever, Jacob was wondering if this boy was really all there, mentally. Did he come across a mentally challenged kid in the woods? Did he fall and have a head injury or something? Jacob asked him, "Son, would it be alright if I looked at your head? I think you may have had an injury."

"My head does hurt…go ahead sir," he said.

Jacob walked over to Thomas to remove his cap and put his hand on the boy's head. His hand passed right through the figure.

What the…Jacob thought. He tried again. Same thing. His hand went right through the figure even though he could plainly see him.

"Either I'm losing my mind or…you're a real ghost…from the Civil War," Jacob whispered to himself. He sat down in front of the boy and stared into his eyes.

Jacob then asked, "Thomas, I think you better tell me what happened. I need to understand and I want to help you, but I don't know how."

"Well, sir," Thomas started, "We were standing at arms waiting for our orders to come from the Major General…when…"

"Wait, who was waiting, where?" Jacob asked.

"All of us cadets from VMI, all 257 of us. The Confederate Army was trying to hold ground at New Market against the Yanks and Major General Breckinridge realized he needed more help," Thomas explained. "He called us up to make the charge."

"And charge you did?" asked Jacob.

"Of course, sir! It was our duty. We were soldiers for the Confederate Army fighting for our own independence!" Thomas said proudly.

"And do you remember if you were injured?" asked Jacob.

"Yes, I was. Five cadets...died that day. Five more in the days to come," Thomas said sadly. "I think I had a head injury...I don't remember too clearly."

"Thomas," Jacob said carefully. "I think you may have died that day also."

"NO SIR I DID NOT!" he exclaimed. Then after he sat and thought for a minute, he said quietly, "Now I remember, I died three days later...at 3:40am."

"3:40am?" Jacob said with a surprise. "I've been awakened every night at 3:40am since I got here. Was it you? Have you been following me?"

"Yes sir," replied Thomas. "I don't know why, but I was drawn to you and I've been following looking for answers."

Jacob looked at him with a concerned, passionate look and asked, "Looking for what, Thomas? What are you looking for?"

Thomas looked up at Jacob with tears and said, "I don't know where I'm supposed to be. I feel lost and can't find my family or friends. I occasionally see other souls wandering around and lately a little boy that sometimes walks with me and keeps me company."

Jacob suddenly knew that this cadet, for some reason, had not crossed over to the other side yet and for some reason was left searching the hills, looking for an answer. Maybe Thomas still had something to complete before he could be released from his captivity here on earth. Jacob instantly realized his mission and maybe the real reason he was here on this Trail in the first place. The only way for Thomas to find his answer was to find out as much from him as possible to help him cross over. And, maybe the little boy that Thomas sometimes sees, too.

Before long, the sun was peeking over the horizon. Thomas looked out and said, "I have to go now."

"Wait," said Jacob. "I've got so much to ask you. Will you come back tonight? Should I stay in this shelter or will you still follow me if I leave?"

"Yes sir, I'll come back tonight," Thomas said. "I can find you wherever you go. You know the time."

Thomas walked outside and headed to the edge of the trees. He turned, looked at Jacob and smiled, then disappeared. Jacob stood staring with tears in his eyes, knowing this was certainly not a dream. He turned and walked into the shelter to pack his gear.

Chapter Six

Jacob had plenty to think about while walking the Trail today. Obviously, Thomas was all over his mind, trying to determine his reason for still being earthbound. He knew he wouldn't rest until he helped this boy find his final destination, a place where Thomas would feel at ease and hopefully be with his family and friends again. Perhaps even his grandfather, Thomas Jefferson.

Yes, Thomas was really the grandson of Thomas Jefferson, the man who was the third President of the United States from 1801 to 1809. Jacob wondered what President Jefferson would've thought, seeing his own grandson fight for independence *against* the Union, the very government that was run by the boy's grandfather.

When Abraham Lincoln became the elected

President in 1860, he campaigned against the expansion of slavery beyond the states in which it already existed. Seven Southern states declared their secession from the Union before Lincoln took office in 1861. Both the outgoing and incoming US administrations rejected the legality of secession and therefore considered it a rebellion. The seven Southern states formed their own Confederate Army to fight against the Union Army of the North. Part of a family lived in a Southern state while part of the same family may have lived in a Northern state, thus becoming an actual brother against brother war. Thomas found himself fighting for the South, believing they had every right to pull away from the Union Government and govern themselves with their own beliefs. President Lincoln and the government of the United States thought otherwise.

As history shows, battles during the war were brutal and fierce. They went on for four, long years, the casualties numbering over 620,000 men and boys. The Confederate Army of the South eventually surrendered to the Union Army of the North on April 9, 1865. Five days later, President Abraham Lincoln was assassinated.

Jacob hiked past Lewis Mountain, then shortly was upon Piney Mountain. Elevations dropped about sixteen-hundred feet from where he stayed at Bear Fence Mountain and the weather had cleared to a beautiful, deep blue sky. The Trail was still quite muddy in some areas, but Jacob knew that by mid-day, they would be mostly dry where the sun beat down on them.

As he approached South River, he passed a large campground filled with family campers. It looked like Family Day or something; he never saw so many families in one wilderness area before. The playground is where most of the smaller kids and mothers were gathered and the majority of dads were busy barbequing and carrying on in friendly conversation with each other. The aroma of roasting hot dogs, burgers, chicken and just about anything you could think of permeated the air and Jacob found himself instantly getting hungry.

A convenient-sized General Store stood at the campground's bordering edge, where campers and hikers could find groceries, snacks, firewood, cold drinks and ice. Jacob walked inside and bought a few things to replenish his supply before getting back on the Trail, including beef jerky and energy bars for snacks.

While he hiked by the park area where the barbequing was taking place, Jacob thought he heard a boy's voice nearby say, "Dad! I think that's my Science teacher!"

"I doubt that," said the man.

The boy then yelled, "Mr. Wizard!"

Jacob looked over and saw Brady Cooper, one of his students from the past school year, looking in his direction smiling in surprise.

"Well, well, well," said Jacob. "Hello, Coop! You travel a long way for class, don't you?"

Brady and his dad laughed. "Hello, Mr. Allen," Brady's dad said surprisingly. "You just can't get away from your students, can you?"

"I always hate the end of the school year," replied Jacob, "because I know I won't see the kids for quite a while. This is a real treat for me."

Mr. Cooper looked at Jacob and asked, "You hungry? I'm just about done barbequing these bratwurst and chicken legs. Got plenty if you care to join us."

Jacob could feel his mouth salivate.

"Well, if you're sure you don't mind. That sounds a heck of a lot better than my jerky and energy bar."

"We'd be honored, Mr. Wizard," said Brady.

"Honored, huh?" said Jacob. "You make me sound like Royalty."

Just then, Brady's mom and little sister, Laura, came walking back from the playground. Mrs. Cooper saw Jacob and said, "Oh my God, Mr. Allen! What a surprise to see you here!"

"Hi, Mrs. Cooper. I'll travel just about anywhere for a good lunch," Jacob said chuckling.

"You came to the right place then," she said laughing.

They all proceeded to sit at the picnic table and load up their plates with the sausages, chicken legs, potato salad, coleslaw and baked beans. A perfect picnic lunch all washed down with cold, refreshing iced tea.

Jacob and the Coopers sat and talked for about an hour when Jacob looked at his watch and said, "I really need to get back on the Trail. I still have quite-a-ways to go today before my next destination for the night. I can't thank you enough for this great meal and company."

"It was our pleasure," said Mr. Cooper. "You need a good meal once in a while to hike the distances you want to travel. Good luck and be careful."

"Thanks," said Jacob. "And special thanks to you, Coop, for noticing me walking by. You made my day."

At Swift Run Gap, the elevation climbed back up to 2,365 feet, a prelude to reaching Hightop at 3,587 feet. There were areas that broke out of the timber into large grasslands, making the views spectacular. Approaching Jacob, near 4pm, was a Boy Scout Troop, consisting of two men and eight boys. The boys looked as if to be about twelve years old, each boy carrying his own backpack.

Jacob was taking a break while sitting on a large rock next to the Trail when one of the gentlemen said, "Good afternoon. What a day, huh?"

"Terrific," he said. "Quite a group you got there."

"It's our five-day summer expedition," the man said. "We do it every year. The boys love it."

"Well, you couldn't have picked a better place," Jacob replied smiling. As the group continued walking by, Jacob noticed one boy had a remarkable resemblance to Jimmy. He was a little older, but the features and blond hair were the same. Jacob smiled and immediately thought of the times that he, Jimmy and Annie had hiking and camping together as a family. He was saddened, but able to keep his smile as they passed.

After they were out of sight, Jacob hoisted his backpack on and headed down the Trail towards Black Rock, his destination for the night.

Over the next few hours, Jacob was energetic and making great time. Anticipating Thomas's arrival later that night made him feel excited and yearning to learn more about his new spirit friend. Before long, he passed Smith Roach Gap, Bacon Hollow and Flattop Mountain. At Simmons Gap, there was another General Store for supplies, but Jacob figured he got enough of them back at South River when he stopped and had that incredible lunch.

Reaching the Loft Mountain Information Center, he asked if there were shelters at or near Black Rock. One of the clerks said there was one, but it was a popular site and usually crowded. Jacob figured this was going to become one of those nights he had to spend in his tent.

People often complain that the AT in Shenandoah Park is too crowded. What they really mean is that there are not too many hikers for the shelters, but there are not enough shelters for the hikers. There are about two-hundred-and-forty shelters, huts or lean-tos along the entire 2,175-mile Appalachian Trail, but only eight huts are within the one-hundred mile Shenandoah Park. On average, you can find shelter about every ten miles, but sometimes it can be much farther. The chance of spending the night alone in a hut or shelter is slim and you'll usually be sharing it with some brand-new acquaintances.

At 7pm, he passed Dundo Group Camp which was filled to capacity. Jacob knew that Black Rock was only a couple of miles further and he was worried that the overflow of campers here had trickled to the shelter where he hoped to spend the night.

When he finally reached the shelter in the early evening, surprisingly, there was no one around yet. Jacob welcomed the solitude, hoping there would be no visitors wanting to spend the night, all the while knowing he would have his ghostly company arriving at 3:40am. Black Rock Shelter is built out of stone, very different from the other shelters. It had a nicely built slanted roof, shingled, with a front porch the full length of the shelter. With two windows on the front side, a door sitting between the two of them, it was airy and looked sturdy as a pillar of rock. This one had two bunk beds at each end with a large table and six chairs in the middle. Being the largest hut he's come across so far, it easily slept eight, ten if you crammed them in. Shelving on the back wall made it convenient for Jacob to arrange his goods from his pack. Down the hill was a nearby spring and Jacob easily gathered water for cooking and drinking, even a sponge bath.

After bathing, Jacob gathered a large pile of assorted firewood for a campfire. He wanted enough wood for the fire to last all night, knowing that's where he and Thomas would be involved in deep conversation until daybreak. Red spruce trees with a clearing in front that held the fire pit surrounded the shelter. He arranged the wood in the fire pit in a teepee fashion to burn quickly and efficiently, and then lit the small kindling to start the fire. As dusk approached, he had a solid burning campfire that was warm and friendly.

Dinner was cooked and consumed, though Jacob's appetite was light, partly because of the big lunch and partly because of being nervous of what was about to happen later on in the evening. Jacob relaxed by the fire, propped up against a tree stump with a cup of tea. It was only 10pm and he knew he had a long wait before Thomas arrived. He also knew there was no way he could get any sleep anticipating Thomas's arrival, so he made more tea and kept the fire going.

Hours passed and Jacob couldn't wait to learn more about Thomas's ordeal, what had happened that fateful day at New Market and what was keeping him here instead of moving on into the afterlife. He prayed that he could somehow help this boy get out of his own Hell and get to Heaven, or wherever he was supposed to go.

He found himself nervously looking at his watch about ten times every hour. The night dragged on and on and it seemed that Thomas's time would never come. At 2am, Jacob said aloud, "Thomas, if you're around, you don't have to wait until 3:40. You're welcome to come now if you can."

Minutes passed with no sign of Thomas. The minutes turned into a long hour. Nothing. Now, just after 3am, Jacob was getting restless and waited impatiently.

A short time more passed when he looked at his watch again - 3:38am. Jacob set his cup of tea down and stood up looking around the area. He listened, but heard nothing. He looked again - 3:39.

"C'mon," he said quietly to himself. "Hurry up."

Jacob stared at his watch as it changed from 3:39 to 3:40. He listened, and looked. Branches across the clearing in front of him rustled. Jacob's heart pounded, hoping it wasn't a bear. Coming out of the spruce, Thomas walked forward. Jacob smiled and Thomas smiled back.

"Welcome, my friend," Jacob said in a relieving manor. "Come and sit by the fire."

Thomas walked over and sat next to Jacob. He looked exactly as the night before, wet and covered with mud even though it had not been raining all day.

"I've been thinking, Thomas. A lot. For some reason, you're stuck in something like a time warp, not able to escape," Jacob said. "We need to find out why and get you home where you belong."

Thomas looked at him confused and said, "Time warp? But it's 1864."

"No, Thomas, it's not 1864. It's 2017."

"What?" Thomas asked. "That can't be, sir. I just

died."

"Thomas, listen to me," Jacob replied. "You died over a hundred-and-fifty years ago. You've been wandering and looking for answers for a hundred-and-fifty years."

"A hundred-and-fifty years?" Thomas asked. His eyes welled up with tears. "I just want to find my family."

"And I promise I'll help you Thomas," Jacob said looking into his eyes. "We'll get you home. Tell me as much as you can remember. I'll be here for you as long as it takes."

"You're a good man, Mr. Jacob, sir," replied Thomas.

"It's just Jacob. Call me Jacob. No need for sir. I'm not your commanding officer. I'm your friend, Thomas."

"Okay…Jacob," said Thomas awkwardly. "Where should I start?"

Jacob thought for a moment and said, "How about telling me what happened at the battle at New Market? Let's start there."

Thomas looked down and thought for a moment, then looked up and spoke.

"It was a miserable day. It had been raining for

days and everything was a mess."

"That's why you look the way you do," Jacob said. "Wet and covered in mud, even though today was perfectly sunny and dry. That's how you looked when you fought in the battle and died."

Thomas nodded and realized that Jacob really understood the situation. He continued with his story.

"It was the Confederate Army's duty to protect and keep control of New Market. The Yankees were trying to take it over to gain control of the Shenandoah Valley. Control of the Valley was critical."

"It sounds like it was quite a task," Jacob said.

"It was," said Thomas. "We were outnumbered and the Yanks had artillery. They were firing cannons at us and we couldn't do anything about it."

"Then what happened?" asked Jacob.

"Well, our Army was getting beaten down badly when Major General Breckinridge realized it was a lost cause without more help," Thomas explained. "He didn't want to, but he made the call for us 257 cadets to charge the artillery line when they were reloading the cannons. We ran down the hill and across the muddy field, shooting and screaming at the Yanks."

"You seem so young, were you in other battles?"

asked Jacob.

"None of us cadets saw battle before that day," replied Thomas.

"And how did you get injured? Do you remember?"

Thomas paused, visibly shaken and upset talking about it and said, "Cannon fire was exploding everywhere. When the Yanks started the reload, we charged, but rifle fire continued. My best friend charging next to me went down; I could see he got hit. He laid there screaming while his stomach poured out blood, mixing with the mud. I reached down and threw his arm over my shoulder to drag him out of danger. That's when something hit my head and I went down."

"Did the cadet charge work?" asked Jacob. "I mean, did you guys get control of the town?"

"We did," said Thomas. "At the expense of many, including five cadets that day. My friend was one of them."

"And what happened to you?" asked Jacob.

"Well, I remember laying there holding my head in the rain and mud," he said. "The pain was terrible, there was a loud ringing in my ears, but I could still hear the rifle fire going on. The cannons started again, exploding everywhere. I heard men screaming and crying all around me. Then I reckon I passed out or something because I woke up later in a military hospital tent."

"You woke up?" Jacob asked. "That's usually a pretty good sign after a head injury. What happened then?"

"Severe infection. I heard them say it was probably from the manure in the muddy farm field where I laid," Thomas said. "It got into my head wound and immediately caused an infection. I was dead in three days."

Jacob looked at him and compassionately said, "In my eyes you're a hero, Thomas. You tried to save the life of your friend and were wounded in the process. To me, that should've been your ticket to Heaven right there."

"I guess God didn't think so," he said sadly.

"There's got to be another reason you're still here," replied Jacob. "God is not finished with you yet. He must've had a future master plan for you all along. There's another reason, Thomas, believe me. We need to find out what that is and get you home, son."

Before long, the night had come to a close and

dawn was upon them. With Thomas arriving at 3:40am, it didn't really leave more than a couple of hours to talk. Thomas stood and politely bid his farewell until the next evening. He walked into the spruce and was gone.

Chapter Seven

Jacob was exhausted, physically and mentally, from hiking all the previous day and getting no sleep for two nights. Talking with Thomas until dawn left him drained of energy and he knew that he needed to get some rest or he wouldn't make it another night. He decided to stay at Black Rock Shelter for one more night and try to sleep all day long. Hopefully, he'd be alone for another night so Thomas would return and continue their talk.

Jacob immediately fell into a deep sleep, waking occasionally and wondering for a moment if last night was all a dream or really happened. He knew it was real, but had to question himself often to make sure. In the early afternoon, he awoke to the sound of the wind picking up and distant rumbles of thunder. Apparently, another storm was heading his way and he was thankful he stayed in the shelter for another day. The Park rules actually prohibit hikers from staying consecutive nights in the same shelter because there are so many people hiking the Trail, but Jacob was hoping a Ranger wouldn't come by and question him or other hikers report him.

By 4pm, the storm had arrived, bringing a hard, steady rain and a lot of thunder and lightning. Jacob was awake, but still wrapped in his sleeping bag when he heard an array of voices getting near the shelter. Six hikers, all college-aged boys, were quite loud and obnoxious as they approached the shelter. Jacob knew they were planning to bunk down there for the night. But he also knew if they did, his chances to talk with Thomas again that night were zero. College boys don't usually sleep much, especially when they're out camping or hiking. He realized they would probably take over the shelter and be laughing and noisy the entire night, keeping Thomas at bay and not making himself known. Jacob, thinking quickly, exited his sleeping bag and splashed a little water over his face, then opened the door and looked out as the boys entered the clearing out front.

"Hey man," one of the boys shouted out upon

seeing Jacob. "Got room in there for six more and gear?"

"I do," replied Jacob as they drew near, "if you don't mind sharing with a guy with a nasty fever and throwing up all day. C'mon in and make yourself cozy."

The boys stopped short and looked at Jacob, his face wet from what they thought was the fever and said to him, "You look awful dude, but we're pretty tough. I think we can handle a little fever."

This wasn't going as planned. Jacob thought for a moment and said, "Then c'mon in out of that pouring rain, just give me a minute to sweep the puke off the floor and make some room for you guys."

The boys froze and stared as if Jacob had the plague or something.

"Well, it's still early, I think we'll just head up to the next shelter a few more miles and let you get your rest," one said, and they turned and couldn't get away fast enough.

Jacob closed the door and chuckled while towel drying his face and hair. "Well, I must say, that worked pretty well," he thought.

The rain ceased by 6pm and he was getting hungry, so he decided to make something to eat while the weather took a break. The front porch on the shelter was slightly protected by a four-foot overhang that was a continuation of the slanted roof over the main hut. Jacob set up his little camp stove on the porch beneath the overhang and was shielded from the dripping rain coming from the trees above. The only sound in the woods at this moment was the hissing of his portable camp stove. He set a small pot of water on the single burner and while he waited for the water to boil, he searched through his food bag for something tasty to cook. A package of freeze-dried, chicken chili caught his eye and that sounded wonderful on a rainy evening. Minutes later, the water was boiling furiously and Jacob poured the hot water into the pouch of dried chili. It took about seven minutes to hydrate every morsel of beans and chicken in the bag and while that was setting up, he broke off a large chunk of sourdough bread from the loaf he bought at the last supply store. The remaining hot water went into his coffee cup with a packet of instant coffee and he soon found himself sitting on the edge of the porch, enjoying his backwoods meal.

With all the rain during the day, there really was no chance of having any kind of a campfire tonight; being that everything around was saturated. Jacob knew that tonight's visit from Thomas would have to take place inside the shelter, or at least on the front porch where it was dry. He also knew that at any time, other hikers could still arrive to spend the night and ruin his chance of continually meeting with Thomas and trying to get to the bottom of his ordeal, possibly setting his spirit free.

By dusk, the sky had cleared, the temperature had dropped and the dampness from the rain left an uncomfortable chill in the air. Jacob put on a long-sleeved flannel shirt and a sweatshirt over top, feeling more at ease with the warmth. He knew tonight would be cold for him sitting on the porch waiting for Thomas and no fire to take the chill out of his bones. Hot tea and coffee were the only remedies prescribed for comfort.

Around 9:45pm, voices were heard coming from the Trail. Jacob couldn't tell who it was or how many, but it appeared he was going to have company tonight in the shelter anyway. A few minutes later, part of that company arrived in the clearing and was heading right for him.

"Oh...hello!" said the young man. "I didn't see you sitting there, man. Been a long day. Is it possible you have any room in there for my wife and me tonight?"

Jacob looked around but only saw the man…no wife.

"Is she in your pocket or something? I don't see her."

The man smiled, "She's back there having the dog take a shit."

"Dog?" Jacob asked. "You have a dog, too?"

"Oh yeah. Our black lab, Shiloh," the man said. "You'll love him."

Great, Jacob thought. A wet dog sleeping with us in the extremely small condominium. Jacob then said, "Shiloh? That's a cool name. Civil War buff?"

"Love the Civil War history," he said. "We live near Richmond, Virginia. A lot of war history there, really all over around here. Don't know what it takes to be a buff, but if it means liking and knowing a lot about something…then I guess I'm a buff. Oh…sorry…my name's Parker."

He stretched out his hand and offered to shake.

"Hi Parker, I'm Jacob," as he shook his hand. "A pleasure."

Just then, a big, black blob of an animal came

bolting out of the trees heading right for them. Jacob was startled and thought it was a bear, quickly jumping back into the shelter.

"Whoa!" Parker yelled. "Shiloh…sit."

Jacob suddenly realized it was the black lab, not a black bear. Shiloh was a five-year-old Black Labrador Retriever with superb Royal Canadian bloodlines that the couple acquired through a high-end breeding service. He was well trained, very muscular and weighed about a hundred pounds, not the kind of dog you would want to have pissed at you.

Parker's wife appeared out of the trees and approached the two men standing at the shelter… along with the dog.

"Okay, he's good for the night," she said. "I buried it."

"Honey," Parker said, "This is Jacob. This is my wife, Diane. He says he has room…wait…you didn't say, did you? I'm sorry, do you have any room in there for us tonight? I didn't even ask if you were alone."

Parker was probably in his late thirties, seems like that was the age of just about every adult Jacob was running into on the Trail, tall, maybe six-foot-one or two, athletic looking. He had medium brown hair, a little shaggy and thick, along with a well-trimmed mustache. Jacob could tell he had a great personality and liked to talk. He seemed at ease with Jacob immediately and just knew people liked him.

Diane also appeared to be in her mid-to-late thirties, about five-foot-six, very attractive. Her hair was dark, almost black, midway down her back and tied in a bushy ponytail. Her eyes were dark as night, but very sexy and sultry looking.

"Yes, of course I have room," Jacob said. "And I'm travelling alone. Not even a dog."

They all chuckled while Jacob patted Shiloh. The lab was very friendly and appeared to love Jacob instantly.

"C'mon, step inside and set up any way you want," Jacob insisted. "I just have one bunk and a little spot on the table for some of my gear."

While unpacking they all had great conversation with each other.

Parker chimed in, "So…Jacob…what kind of work do you do?"

"I'm a Science teacher in a school near Detroit," he said. "This seemed like a good therapeutic trip to take on my time off."

"Therapeutic huh?" Parker asked. "Therapeutic because…it's pretty rough there, isn't it? All those kids on the loose in the city…parents don't give a crap about them…if they even have any parents to speak of…burning this, burning that, drug deals, no adult supervision or sense of direction whatsoever. Something like that?"

"Not exactly that in my case," Jacob responded. "You seem to know quite a bit about kids and school. How's that?"

"Guidance Counselor at a high school," Parker said. "Richmond is bad too. I suppose it's everywhere near the big cities."

"He brings a lot of it home with him," Diane said. "It's so hard not to. Many of the kids are combative…they don't want direction from anyone or be told what they can and cannot do. They think they already know everything. But those few that realize they need help…and they really want help…it's heartbreaking. You can't help but bring it home."

Parker reached into his backpack and pulled out a large bottle. He unscrewed the cap and poured the liquid into Diane's cup, Jacob's cup and then his own.

"What's this?" Jacob asked.

"Blackberry brandy. It comes on all of our trips. It's the first thing I pack in my bag. It's ritual," Parker said.

He raised his cup and offered a toast. "To life. And the kids."

Jacob paused, thinking about Annie and Jimmy, then they all raised and tipped their cups together and drank.

Parker immediately refilled the cups. Jacob thought this was pretty cool, a nice couple sharing their prized hiking possession with a total stranger. He knew they were sincere and thoughtful people. They raised their cups again, nothing was said, just looked into each other's eyes and drank. Once again, Parker refilled the empty cups.

"So, Jacob...why is this therapeutic for you, if you don't mind me asking?" asked Parker.

Jacob thought for a moment, thinking he didn't want to burden strangers with his problems, but then realized it really was therapeutic to just talk about it...which he really hadn't done much with anyone, and this guy's job was listening to people with problems as a Guidance Counselor...and as a friend. He's not there to tell him what to do, he's there to listen. Maybe he was brought here to help him heal...all part of the process. It's always in God's hands, His plan for each of us. Jacob had to accept it and trust it.

"Well...okay. I actually feel very comfortable with you two. I mean three," Jacob said smiling, looking at Shiloh. "And this brandy is helping too...I'm sure."

"You had a tragedy occur in your life, didn't you?" asked Diane.

"What makes you say that?" asked Jacob surprisingly. "Am I that transparent?"

"Diane is a spirit sensitive...she senses things from the spirit world and feels very strong emotions from certain people. You must be one of those people."

"Wow...really?" Jacob asked. "A spirit sensitive...I've never...met someone like that before. How does that work? I mean...oh...I don't know what I mean."

"I've been aware of this feeling since I was a little girl," she said. "I don't know why...I quit asking. It's just there. I don't control it. If the feelings are strong, there's something going on and I know it."

"And you got those feelings being around me?" asked Jacob.

"Big time," she said. "As soon as we walked into

the shelter together. But I wanted the evening to play out a little more before saying anything."

"So…how does it work?"

"It doesn't work, it just happens. It's a feeling of energy that I sense," she said. "The human body and soul are a form of energy, and it gives off energy. Albert Einstein said, 'Energy cannot be destroyed; it can only be changed from one form to another.' That's why it's believed that spirits are a form of energy, changed from body to spirit, because the soul's energy can't be destroyed. It's these spirit energies that I can sense, along with strong emotional energies."

"You're a Science teacher Jacob, I'm sure you knew that," said Parker.

"Uh…yeah…I did. I mean, I knew about Einstein and his theories and all," said Jacob. "But I guess I never put it in that perspective before."

He thought for a moment, staring outside into the darkness.

"I think I'm beginning to understand something a little more now," Jacob said still looking outside. "About energies. Thanks for opening my eyes a little wider."

"Okay Jacob…back to you," said Parker. "Diane

revealed she sensed you may have had a tragedy or something in your life. Care to talk about it, man? There's nobody here but Diane and me. And Shiloh. But I promise he won't tell anybody."

"Well, if dogs have spirits and energies too…you can't guarantee that statement," Jacob said jokingly.

Parker and Diane smiled. "Point made," said Parker. "C'mon Jacob, this may be part of your therapeutic journey. It's a healing process."

Jacob sipped his brandy once more.

"Okay. You're right. And Diane seems to be very good at what she does," said Jacob. "She is absolutely right. There was a tragedy in my life. About eight years ago. I lost my wife and son to a drunk driver."

Diane gasped. Parker leaned forward and touched Jacob's hand. Jacob knew it was a sincere touch; one that a best friend would offer.

"Oh my God Jacob…I'm so sorry," Diane said with a heartbroken voice.

Even animals can sense certain things about people or surroundings. Jacob was obviously distraught and hung his head low, tears starting to well in his eyes. Shiloh came over, sat next to Jacob and laid his head in Jacob's lap as if to comfort him. Jacob couldn't help but smile and patted Shiloh's head.

"Is this dog a spirit sensitive too?" Jacob asked jokingly.

"He's smarter than people give him credit for," said Parker. "Continue, please."

For the next hour, Jacob poured out his thoughts, his feelings, his anger, his resentment, his love, his bitterness, and most of all…his guilt. He just couldn't get over the idea that if he had been there with his family, together, things would be different and none of it would've happened. He continued to blame himself for the death of his family.

Of course, Parker and Diane tried to convince him it was ridiculous to blame himself, that it wasn't his fault at all and bad things just happen whether we understand it or not, even to good people, but Jacob could not be convinced otherwise. He was shocked that he finally was able to express his thoughts and feelings to someone, strangers that they were, but he felt at ease with them and had no problem saying what needed to be said. He also soon realized that his new friends would make it difficult, if not impossible, to meet with Thomas later as planned. Jacob's thoughts once again turned to helping Thomas. He needed to find out more and hopefully Thomas wouldn't be discouraged or feel threatened by the presence of other people and just walk away and never return.

It was just after midnight when everyone decided to finally settle in for the night. Parker took Shiloh out for one last moment of relief while Diane arranged their sleeping bags and the dog's blanket near them. Jacob's head was spinning a little from the brandy and he knew he'd fall asleep quickly, hopefully to be awakened by Thomas's presence later.

"Thanks for opening up to us, Jacob," Diane said sincerely. "I know it was hard…and still is."

"Thanks for coaxing me. You're good people. Really. Thank you."

Parker and Shiloh walked in and soon everyone was tucked in their bags, including the dog on his own blanket.

"Parker?" said Jacob inquisitively.

"Yes Jacob?" asked Parker.

Jacob paused. "Thank you."

"You don't have to thank anyone. You would've done the same, my friend," said Parker. "Caring people care for people."

Jacob smiled. "That's a great quote. Who said

that?"

"I just did," said Parker chuckling.

"See you in the morning guys. And you too, Shiloh."

Shiloh looked up at Jacob and wagged his tail.

"Goodnight, Jacob," said both Parker and Diane.

Jacob awoke to a noise. He glanced over and Shiloh already had his head up growling a low, deep growl. Parker and Diane looked over and Parker whispered, "What's up, boy? Something out there?"

Shit. Jacob knew it had to be Thomas. How was he going to go out and meet with him for a couple of hours without any suspicion? This wasn't good, he thought.

Shiloh stood up and growled again. A deeper growl.

"I'll go check it out," said Parker.

"No...I'll go," insisted Jacob. "Stay here with your wife. She needs you." Jacob was afraid that Parker would scare Thomas off. He needed to go himself and possibly explain the situation to him, hopefully to get Thomas to come back tomorrow night when they were gone.

"Okay...but be careful," warned Parker. "You don't know what's out there."

"I have a pretty good idea," said Jacob. "I'll be fine."

Parker looked at him with a puzzled look on his face, then looked at Diane and whispered, "How the hell could he know what's out there?"

Jacob walked out the door, Shiloh's growl getting intense now. It seemed the dog was warning him of danger and didn't like him going out there. Jacob looked down and said, "Easy boy. It's okay." He closed the screen door behind him, keeping Shiloh inside.

"Jacob, please be careful," Diane whispered. "Don't do anything stupid."

He looked around the clearing...nothing could be seen in the dim moonlight. Jacob stepped off the porch, hoping to find Thomas off to the side somewhere. He started to walk toward the scrub trees surrounding the clearing. As he approached the far side, he heard a twig snap. Shiloh barked from inside the shelter. Jacob knew Thomas was within reach and needed to speak with him quietly. He turned his head back towards the shelter and said, "I'm okay, guys; I don't see anything out here."

While looking back at the shelter he heard another noise in front of him. Quietly, he whispered, "Thomas?"

Shiloh went into a barking rage. He sensed danger and needed to let Jacob know, but all Jacob could do was be angry that he couldn't speak with Thomas. He turned back towards the scrub trees and...standing four feet in front of him...not Thomas...but a huge, black bear, staring him in the face.

Jacob froze. The humungous bear snarled and let out a deep growl making Jacob nearly pass out. He started slowly walking backwards; the bear started to follow. Shiloh couldn't take anymore and lunged through the screen door, tearing towards the bear. The bear stood up on its hind legs and showed his true size. He was towering above Jacob. As the dog got close, Shiloh barked and snapped at the bear. The bear swiped at Shiloh a couple of times, missing...and finally realizing the dog wouldn't let up, he ran off into the woods. Jacob fell backwards on his butt and sat there in shock. Shiloh came up and licked his face relentlessly.

"My God, man, are you okay? Are you hurt?" Parker said while running out to him.

"Uh...yeah...okay...I mean...no...I don't think I'm hurt, I'm okay," said Jacob while checking himself. Realizing he was untouched, he said happily, "Except for this sloppy, dog slobber all over my face."

"That dog slobber saved your life, man," said Parker. "You can bet he'll be on guard the rest of the night...especially since there's no good screen door anymore. I'll report it when we get back so the AT crews can repair it."

Jacob wiped his face, stood up and they went back to the shelter. Diane propped open what was left of the screen door and said mildly, "That's why we bring Shiloh on these trips. I can't tell you how many times he's scared off animals. Even other hikers that appear to be shady. He senses trouble when we can't. He's our protector."

"It seems like all I've done is thank you guys since I met you," said Jacob apologetically. "I don't know what would've happened if you weren't here."

"I do," said Parker. "You'd be dead and a tasty bear appetizer...and not necessarily in that order."

Jacob suddenly cringed at the thought of being

eaten alive...screaming, kicking, while the flesh and meat was being ripped off your body while you were still conscious. A lot of reality went through his mind in just a few seconds.

They walked back into the shelter, talked about it for a while until their heart rates finally settled down and then crawled back into their sleeping bags, Shiloh now laying down in front of the door keeping guard and watching outside in case the bear returned. Before long, they fell back asleep, eventually even the dog.

Shiloh's head raised...looking outside, he growled lightly. Jacob was dozing when he heard the dog growl. He looked over at Parker and Diane, they hadn't moved yet. Shiloh's light growl turned into more like a whimper and he was wagging his tail. With still no movement from across the shelter, Jacob looked at the dog and whispered, "What is it boy?"

Shiloh stood up and looked at him, then outside. Jacob looked at his watch. It was 3:40am.

Dammit, he thought to himself. He knew he couldn't get up without drawing attention. He laid there looking out the screen for some kind of sign of Thomas, but could only see darkness. Shiloh turned his head to the right as if he spotted something outside, then whimpered a little, wagging his tail a little harder. A faint vision of Thomas appeared at the clearing.

"Easy boy," whispered Jacob. Shiloh looked at him, cocking his head as if confused. "It's okay…he's a friend."

Thomas stood there motionless; looking at the shelter, knowing Jacob had company. He waited.

Diane started to rustle. Jacob could see her moving about and trying not to disturb her husband sleeping in the bunk below her. She looked over and saw Jacob awake.

She whispered, "Jacob, what's going on?"

"Nothing. The dog thought he heard something. There's nothing there. Go back to sleep."

She put her head down. She was lying on her back looking straight up at the ceiling. The dog was still looking outside, wagging his tail. Thomas continued to wait.

Suddenly, Diane spoke. "I can feel him."

Jacob looked at her a little shocked, feeling nervous now, and asked, "You can feel who?"

"I don't know…but there's somebody out there nearby. I can feel his spirit."

"You mean a dead person?" he asked.

"Of course I mean a dead person. It's their spirit energy I feel…and I feel him now." She turned on her side to look out the screen. Parker rolled over and suddenly woke up.

"What's going on?" he asked. "Why is everybody up?"

Diane squinted from her bunk to look through the dirty screen, but couldn't see Thomas. Thomas could see everything that was going on and walked away, disappearing into the night. Shiloh's tail stopped wagging and he was silent.

"I don't feel him anymore," she said.

"Feel who?" asked Parker.

"I don't know. I felt someone's spirit nearby and now it's gone."

"Here we go," said Parker. "She feels spirits everywhere. It's a gift. Or maybe it's a curse, I don't know. But those paranormal groups out there? They know about her and want her. It makes for good reality TV, you know man?"

Jacob didn't respond and slumped back into his bunk, staring outside, wondering if that was the last time he was ever going to see Thomas.

Chapter Eight

By early morning, Jacob was already up and about making coffee out at the campfire for everyone. He kept thinking about last night, whether Thomas was gone for good and that he lost his chance to help him. Diane came walking to the fire and sat down next to Jacob on a log that was laid for seating.

"I was watching you from the shelter," she said with a troubled tone. "I can tell something is bothering you. Care to talk about it?"

"Not sure what you're talking about," he said. "I'm fine."

"Jacob, I sensed a spirit nearby last night. I know it was here," she said. "It seems right after I said it was gone you withdrew into yourself. You didn't even acknowledge what I said. And I saw you staring at the ceiling for quite a while after that."

He continued to stare into the campfire, then turned to her and spoke softly, "I was just thinking about my family, that's all."

"I could understand that…if it was the truth," she said knowing differently.

Jacob stared into her eyes, knowing that she was onto something much deeper than he revealed. Just then, Parker flung the screen door open and Shiloh ran out to them all excited. Parker yelled in an alarming, loud voice, "Attention campers! I smell coffee! I hope there's enough left for me!" Diane and Jacob both turned to look at him at the same time, Jacob saying, "Good morning, O Quiet One of the Woods. Of course there's coffee." But he really wanted to say, "Well thanks for breaking the quiet, serious moment, you obnoxious loudmouth."

Diane turned back to Jacob, looking into his eyes, whispering, "I know there's something Jacob. I only hope you can come to terms with it to ease your pain."

"So," said Parker walking over to them, "What have I missed? You two look like you're in deep conversation."

"We were just discussing the episode last night,"

she said, not letting on to anything personal.

"Oh yeah, that big bear," he said chuckling. "Jacob...that was freaking crazy the way you just walked out there not knowing what it was."

"No Parker, not the bear," Diane said. "We were talking about the spirit."

"Oh...yeah...the spirit. Well, I don't know why you're talking about something that wasn't real. That damn black bear was pretty fucking real!" said Parker.

"And so was the spirit," said Diane with a tone. "You know I can feel them. I felt him there, and then I felt him leave."

"What's your take on all of this, Jake?" asked Parker.

"It's Jacob," he said, "Not Jake. I'm going to side with Diane on this because I believe what she feels is true."

"Okay Jacob...and sorry for calling you Jake," he said. "I was just trying to break the mood a little."

Jacob looked at him and smiled.

"It's okay. I guess I didn't sleep much last night," he said. "Just a little testy. It's not your fault."

Parker took a sip of his coffee and said to Diane, "Honey, we better start packing up. We've got some ground to cover before our next stop tonight."

"Okay," she said. "Are you packing up and heading out too, Jacob?"

"Yeah, but I'm going to stay for a little while longer," he replied. "Got some things to sort out...you know?"

Diane looked at him with a loving, caring look. "Yes...I do know."

The couple walked back into the shelter and starting packing. Shiloh chose to move next to Jacob and sit while he pawed at Jacob for attention. Jacob, smiling at the dog and petting his head, stared into Shiloh's eyes and whispered to him, "What the hell do I do now, Shiloh?"

About an hour later, the two exited the shelter, packs bulging with gear and food. Once on the porch, they helped each other get the packs mounted on their backs. Looking at Jacob and Shiloh sitting by the fire, Parker said to Diane, "Looks like each of them found a new friend."

"C'mon Shiloh, time to get moving," Parker yelled softly.

Shiloh looked at Jacob, licked his face as if to

say thanks and came running. Jacob stood up and walked over to the trio. He offered his outstretched hand to Parker to shake.

"Thanks for listening, Parker," Jacob said sincerely grasping his hand. "And for Shiloh chasing that bear away last night, too."

Parker chuckled. "Remember that old Honda motorcycle commercial from the 70's?" he asked. "The catch phrase was, 'You meet the nicest people on a Honda'. Well I think you meet the nicest people on the Trail."

Jacob smiled. "I couldn't agree with you more."

Diane approached and Jacob once again extended his hand in thanks. Diane pushed his hand aside and threw her arms around him for a big hug, whispering in his ear, "Think about what I said. Come to terms with it and ease your pain."

"Thank you," he said emotionally. "I'll do my best."

"Let's get this show on the road!" Parker yelled.

Jacob knelt down and hugged Shiloh too, getting his face licked repeatedly again. They waved goodbye as they walked off onto the Trail, leaving Jacob to his seclusion once again. He knew he had to leave this place and move on to another, hoping Thomas would take a chance on coming back later tonight. Jacob was fearful that would not happen because of the ruckus last night and Thomas just walking away into the darkness. He could only hope and pray it was not the last he'd seen of Thomas.

Jacob slowly walked back to the shelter, periodically looking over his shoulder to see if Thomas was anywhere around, but all was quiet in the deep woods. He couldn't help feeling somewhat depressed as he packed his gear and got ready to move on. Finally, after everything was ready for the Trail again, Jacob sat down in the chair and whispered, "Thomas, if you can hear me…I want you to find me tonight again and come back to talk to me. Please don't be afraid and just disappear. We have so much more to do."

After a moment of pondering his thoughts, Jacob stood up, hoisted his backpack over his shoulders, and walked out the door. Standing on the porch, he looked around the clearing one last time, hoping something would happen and maybe see Thomas, but of course nothing did. Jacob whispered again, "Tonight Thomas…please. Tonight." He stepped off the porch, walked over to the smoldering coals of the campfire and covered them with dirt and sand to smother the remaining embers. He then turned and continued his journey down the Trail.

The morning was bright with sunshine; the Trail was drying out from all the previous rain from days before. Jacob did a lot of thinking while walking, occupying his thoughts as he kept shuffling forward, not really paying much attention to the beauty around him. It seemed to help the miles pass more easily, even though he had no choice but to think about what happened last night. Hours passed without any other hikers coming his way. He thought that seemed a little odd because usually this time of year the Trail is very active with thru hikers and day hikers. The trail, also, seemed to narrow a lot more than usual and thickened with heavy growth and deadfall. Another hour passed before Jacob realized why there were no hikers and the trail had diminished…through all of his thinking and distractions, he made a wrong turn miles back and lost the main Trail completely. He had two choices…turn around and go back the same way he traveled for half a day and end up where he started this morning, completely wasting an entire day of travel, or check his position with the map and compass and try to cut through the wilderness with no trail until he ran into the main Trail. The latter would require some rough terrain to travel, but would cut down his miles considerably. Not wanting to waste an entire day, he decided to blaze his own trail and cut through the thick forests in search of the main Trail.

Jacob's map showed him to be about four miles to the west of the Trail with some pretty rough, rocky outcrops to traverse over, including a stream. He thought to himself, how hard could this really be? I'll just head due east, run into the Trail in a couple of hours, and be back on track. He checked his compass, turned to the east and headed into the thick wilderness, no trail or path in sight.

Another hour-and-a-half had passed and Jacob realized he only traveled about a mile. Bushwhacking through the thick forest was much harder and time consuming than he anticipated. He kept a close watch on his compass heading so as not to get off track again, but the terrain ahead was getting impossible to traverse in a straight line. Jacob had to start making detours around rocks, cliffs and steep slopes, making his "short" detour into a much longer one.

A couple of times, his heading brought him out on a rocky cliff high above the valley. Jacob could see across the Shenandoah Valley and knew he had to get to the other side of that valley to pick up the Trail. He floundered around the cliff's edges until he came upon a cut in the rocks that sliced down and through the rocky outcrop, paving a way for him to start his descent into the lower valley and then up the other side of the ridge to the Trail. Slowly, and carefully, he maneuvered around boulders and downed trees to make his way to lower ground. The terrain was steep and the rocks were slippery in the shaded areas where the sun had not dried up the wetness from the rain. Jacob continually grabbed the rock cliff edges for support to keep from falling down the slope. A slip and tumble here would surely be disastrous with no one around or even a way to contact anyone if he was injured. Something as simple as a twisted ankle could be life threatening in these mountains. Jacob had to be extra careful and cautious with every step.

As he rounded the next turn between the boulders, he grabbed the rock high on his right for support to keep from slipping down the hill. When he looked up, he was face to face with a copperhead snake that was sunning itself on the rock. Copperheads are venomous pit vipers found all over the Appalachian Mountains, but people rarely die from a bite. However, depending on your immune system, they can make you extremely ill and medical attention is essential. When Jacob reached around the corner to grab the rock, he startled the snake and it lunged at him to strike. Jacob quickly jumped back, lost his footing and started to tumble down the slope. Luckily, he only rolled about fifteen feet before hitting a tree that prevented him from rolling much farther. His backpack hit the tree full force, which acted like a cushion and prevented serious injury to his back or body. At least he rolled far enough to get away from the snake without being bitten. He slowly composed himself, rose to his feet and checked for any injuries…including a snakebite. He found nothing. Jacob looked up the hill at the rock where the snake was still coiled looking at him. He chuckled with a laugh of luck and said, "If Annie was here, she'd be grabbing you and stuffing you in her backpack to take home for the classroom. Consider yourself lucky." Although, Jacob really knew that he was the lucky one.

Hours passed before he finally hit the bottom of

the valley where a fast-water river separated him from the other side. The river was about twenty feet across, but moving too quickly to even attempt a crossing without being swept violently downstream. Jacob decided to follow the river to see if the crossing got narrower at some point where he could cross. Tons of boulders of all sizes littered the river and banks, with the water finding its way between rock after rock. Jacob was getting tired of trying to follow the rough riverbank of boulders, so he decided to make an attempt to cross at the narrowest place he could find. That meant trying to leap across from a rock on this side to another on the other side, jumping about seven feet over raging water. The water was thrashing and turbulent in this area and he didn't want to find out what white water surfing would be like bouncing off rocks, so he had to plan his jump carefully.

Jacob decided the best way to get the most out of his jump would be to do it without the backpack. He unclipped the straps and lowered the pack off his back. Grabbing the shoulder strap, he picked it up, swung it back and forth a few times, then launched it with all his strength over the river to the other side. It landed on the bank in a secure place. He was now halfway there.

This time, it was his turn to launch across the river. He saw the rock he needed to land on, a fairly flat rock on the top, and a good jump would carry him to it. Jacob took three steps back, then ran swiftly and jumped across the river to the other side. He landed with both feet on the flat rock, almost like a gymnast would land after jumping off the springboard over the horse to make a perfect landing. He was amazed that he could jump that far and land perfectly on a flat rock.

"Nice job Jacob, I must say," he said proudly to himself.

He then took a step for the bank to retrieve his backpack...the bank was slippery with mud and Jacob's feet slid out from beneath him and down he went...into the river. The raging water quickly captured his body and swept him downstream, rocks and boulders everywhere. Jacob suddenly remembered when he and Annie were whitewater rafting in West Virginia that the instructor told them if you ever fall out of the raft, keep your feet facing forward so you can bounce off the rocks with your feet and not your head. Jacob quickly turned his legs in front of him and it's a good thing he did. He immediately started hitting rocks and boulders, but luckily, was able to keep pushing off with his feet and keep moving downstream. He searched frantically for an eddy of calm water near the shore to get to so he could exit the river before he got too far away from his backpack. After bouncing and floating about a hundred yards, he found his spot and was able to pull himself out of the water. Once again, being beaten and tattered, he looked over his body for any damage or injuries, and luckily found none. Although wet, chilly and exhausted, Jacob found his way back upstream along the bank to his backpack. He then changed into dry clothes and continued, leaving the whitewater behind.

It was becoming quite obvious to him that getting back to the original Trail by sundown was not going to happen. He realized he'd better start looking for a place to set up camp for the night because there were no shelters anywhere to be found in the wilderness he was exploring. Tonight would be a tent night and as rustic as it could be.

Partway up the mountain slope, Jacob came to a rock face about thirty feet high with a small clearing in front of it. The rocks faced to the southwest and were still warm from being in the sun all day. Rocks in the sunlight are known to hold heat for hours after sundown, so camping near these rocks would keep him warm much longer than camping near a stream or hollow that holds the dampness and cold air. He decided to pitch his tent in the small clearing in front of the rock face. Then he built his campfire site up against the rocks, keeping the rocks warm from the fire and expelling heat long into the night after the fire was out. Jacob gathered quite a bit of firewood from the nearby downed trees to last for hours after the sun went down. When he finished setting up camp, he outlined the fire pit with rocks for a barrier to keep the fire from traveling, then stacked his wood in the pit. Dry pine needles work well as a fire starter and he gathered a few handfuls and stuffed them in the center of the woodpile. Striking a match, he lit the pine needles and the fire began to pop and crack. Instantly, a nice fire was roaring. Jacob filled a small pot with water and set it near the fire to boil. He dug through his pack and pulled out his food bag, found a package of Beef Stroganoff and set it aside until the water was ready. A few minutes passed before the water came to a boil, at which time Jacob poured some into the pouch of Stroganoff to hydrate the freeze-dried noodles and beef. He also made himself a cup of hot coffee with the remaining boiling water and sat back with his meal at hand. A chunk of bread from his stash made the meal complete.

The sun was setting over the ridge he previously traversed down into the lower valley and the deep forest was turning to darkness. Birds were becoming quiet and chattering squirrels were silenced as they nestled back into their homes. Deer were starting to arrive nearby for their night play. Twigs snapped around Jacob in the total darkness and every little noise was amplified tenfold in the silent woods. He sat there listening to the wildlife and wondered if he would ever see Thomas again. Not only was there confusion last night with Diane and Parker being at his campsite, but now he's so far off the Trail that he didn't know if Thomas could even find him here. Jacob was feeling sad and depressed that Thomas was gone, left wandering the mountains in search of something that he had no idea what to look for.

The dark, silence of the woods, the sound of the crackling fire and a full belly brought drowsiness to Jacob as he sat there leaning against the warm, rock wall. He thought of his trials from throughout the day...getting off track from the main trail and bushwhacking through the wilderness, nearly getting bitten by a poisonous copperhead snake and tumbling down the slope and hitting a tree, jumping across a raging river only to slip and fall back into the churning water and be swept a hundred yards downstream. Feeling exhausted, relaxed and knowing he was safe; it wasn't long before he drifted off into a deep slumber.

Jacob dreamed while sleeping, things seemed so real as if he was living the thoughts as they happened in his mind. He dreamed of being awakened by the kiss of the warm, morning sun against the right side of his face. It was as if he could actually feel the warmth and gentle breeze on his cheek. Thinking it was morning, he slowly opened his eyes to see the beautiful sunrise.

It was dark. The campfire was giving off a flickering light as it burned down to hot coals. Jacob felt a presence nearby. Now with his eyes open and in darkness, he could still feel what he thought was the warm, morning sun against his right cheek. He slowly moved his eyes to the right, not moving his head or any part of his body.

The head of a large, black bear was only inches from his cheek, the bear's hot breath wafting on his face. Warm, morning sun? No. How about the breath of a vicious, wild animal only inches away from your face. Jacob froze with fear, afraid to even breathe. The bear sniffed him repeatedly as if to size him up for the next meal. Then, the bear turned and walked a few feet away, coming to the food bag that Jacob left out because he was too tired to remember to hang it high in a tree. The bear started to rip the nylon bag apart, dragging out all the food Jacob had tucked inside. Apparently, the bear thought he hit the jackpot, because after seeing all the food pouches, bread and snacks that were spread out like a smorgasbord, he decided to lay down and eat everything in sight. Jacob watched in horror and didn't move an inch, fearing the bear might attack him after the food was gone and also watched as all the survival food he had was being devoured, and not by him. If he survived the bear incident, having no food at all was the next life-threatening issue. Not knowing where he was in relation to the main Trail, Jacob had no idea when he was going to come across another opportunity to get more food from a store along the way. It could be days before that happened, and burning a lot of calories busting through the wilderness would surely take its toll on him.

The bear seemed content after eating all of Jacob's food and snacks. Freeze-dried food expands and swells as it hydrates and since the food wasn't pre-hydrated like Jacob does by adding hot water prior to eating, the dried morsels absorbed the fluids in the bear's stomach after ingested and probably made the bear's stomach stretch and bloat to make him think he was full after eating those pouches. Satisfied, the bear rose to his feet and walked off into the darkness of the forest.

Jacob, still in shock and terrified, continued to sit there afraid to move for another hour-and-a-half for fear the bear might return to have Jacob for dessert. But all was quiet.

Finally, after breathing a sigh of relief and thanking God that he wasn't eaten alive, Jacob crawled into his tent to try to get some sleep. He laid there worrying about when he was going to find some food, let alone find his way out of there tomorrow. He also thought of Thomas and wondered if he would see him later tonight, or never again. He checked his watch...it was 11:45pm. As the adrenaline surge from the excitement wore off, it put him in a relaxed state and he soon surrendered to a deep sleep.

Noises outside. Jacob was awakened to footsteps and rustling outside near the fire pit. That's where the bear laid and ate everything he could find. He's back. The bear is back. He wants more. He knows that this place was a food source…and he's hungry again. Now the only food here is Jacob. Jacob's heart raced, yet he couldn't make a sound for fear the bear would come after him in the tent. All he could do was count down the seconds of his remaining life until the bear slashed the tent open with his sharp claws. He realized that this backpacking trip really wasn't a very good idea. He was hoping it would *change* his life, not *end* it.

More rustling outside. It sounded like the bear was moving the unused firewood logs around, probably looking for more remnants of food. Suddenly, Jacob heard a thud. It sounded like the bear picked up a log and tossed it. Now he's thinking the bear is pissed from finding no food and he's coming after him. Jacob waited in silence, counting the last seconds of his life. For some reason, he looked at his watch, maybe to see the time of his imminent death. It was 3:40am.

3:40am? Wait a minute. Jacob, still cautious and

nervous, slowly unzipped his tent door a few inches to peer outside. Standing next to the fire was not the bear; it was Thomas. The loud thud that Jacob heard, thinking it was the bear being violent and throwing a log, was actually Thomas tossing a log on the fire to get it going again. Jacob unzipped the door the rest of the way and looked out at Thomas. Thomas looked at Jacob and smiled.

"Surprise," he said chuckling.

"Jesus, Thomas!" Jacob exclaimed.

"It's Thomas Garland Jefferson, not Jesus Thomas," said Thomas smiling.

Jacob exited the tent and came out to meet Thomas. They both took a seat next to the fire.

"I'm so glad to see you, Thomas," Jacob said. "For a couple of reasons."

"You thought I wasn't coming back, didn't you?" Thomas said softly.

"I was really worried you got scared off last night because we couldn't talk with other people there," Jacob replied. "And I didn't think you were coming back. I took a wrong turn off the Trail and thought you wouldn't find me."

"Jacob," said Thomas, "I believe it's my mission

to stay with you until we accomplish what needs to be done. I've been drawn to you, for a reason, and I hope we figure this out together."

"I could've used you earlier this evening. I was visited by a hungry black bear," Jacob told Thomas.

"Well, I guess he wasn't THAT hungry," said Thomas. "You're still here."

"Very funny," chuckled Jacob. "He got my food bag and ate everything I had. I don't know what I'm going to do now."

"You're going to eat plants and stuff until you get more food," Thomas told Jacob. "It's called survival."

"But I have no idea what's okay to eat and what's not. I never studied that part of Science," said Jacob.

"I can show you," Thomas replied. "We learned at Cadet School and trained in the wilderness."

Jacob looked perplexed and said to Thomas, "But how can you show me what to eat when you're only here in the middle of the night? I get hungry during the day, you know."

Thomas stood up and walked to the edge of the trees. The campfire was now lighting up the entire area around Jacob's camp.

"Come over here, Jacob. You see this?" Thomas said.

Jacob stood and walked over to Thomas. "Yeah, it looks like minty leaves," Jacob said to Thomas. He reached down to pick a batch.

"DON'T TOUCH IT!" Thomas exclaimed. "That's not mint. It's Common Nettle, or sometimes called Stinging Nettle."

"Stinging Nettle? That doesn't sound very appetizing."

"Oh, it's not," said Thomas. "The stems and leaves have tiny pointed hairs that act like needles. When you touch them, they inject you with an irritating poison that makes your skin break out immediately into bumps and blisters. Very painful."

"How do you know about this?" asked Jacob.

"In our cadet training, the Commanding Officers made us crawl through a field of this horrible stuff," Thomas said grimacing. "Of course, we all immediately broke out in painful blisters and were miserable, the more we scratched the itch, the more it burned and spread."

"Why in the world would your officers put you boys through something like that?" Jacob asked sincerely. "That's just cruel punishment."

"No," replied Thomas. "It toughened us up. They told us as painful as that was; it was nothing compared to what we'd face in battle. They tried to weed out the weaklings so they would end up with the toughest cadets."

"Still sounds cruel to me," said Jacob.

Thomas smiled and said, "All I can tell you is stay away from this stuff. It's not mint."

"Got it," said Jacob.

"And if you're not 100% sure of what plant you're going to eat? Don't eat it," Thomas said sternly. "Some of these things out here can kill you within hours."

Jacob looked at Thomas with confusion.

"So, what can I be 100% sure of to eat to get me by?" asked Jacob.

"Simple," Thomas said with confidence. "Cattails."

"Cattails? They're edible?" asked Jacob.

"And plentiful everywhere this time of year," replied Thomas. "They grow in water and you can pull them out of the muck, rinse them off and eat them raw, root and stem. They have a lot of starch, so be careful not to eat too much. They could give you a stomachache. If you boil them, that'll remove some of the starchy taste and be easier on you."

"So, if I'm going to get sick from it, why would I eat them?"

"It's called survival, Jacob," Thomas said. "These will keep you alive and going until you find better food. If you eat nothing, you'll die."

"Makes sense, I guess," said Jacob.

"They say if you've found cattails, you've already found four out of five survival essentials," Thomas told Jacob.

"I don't understand," said Jacob.

"Look, if you find cattails, here's what you have," explained Thomas. "Water, because they grow in water…food, because you can eat them…shelter, you can make a shelter out of the stalks…and a source of fuel for heat – the dry, old stalks and tinder from the fuzzy tops burn easily. The fifth essential, the only essential out of five required that you're missing…is companionship."

Jacob looked at Thomas and realized this young kid was really trained well for combat and survival.

"There's so many more edible plants out here, but this is all you really need to know right now because

I know you'll find more food somewhere soon," Thomas added. "This will get you through."

Jacob was actually a little excited about trying to eat some cattails, not that he had any choice, but now he knew he could eat something in the wild that grows in marshy areas and is plentiful. He couldn't wait for his gourmet cattail debut.

Thomas then walked over and pointed to a pine tree.

"You see here, Jacob?" asked Thomas, pointing to the needles on the branch.

"I love pine trees, they're my favorite tree," said Jacob. "In fact, the White Pine is Michigan's State Tree."

Thomas looked at Jacob, confused and replied, "What? I don't understand what you're saying."

"Never mind, Thomas, I'm just rambling on."

Giving Jacob a confused look, Thomas pointed back at the pine needles and said, "You can strip the needles off the branch and put them in boiling water. They make a very healthy pine tea that helps to give you energy and has healing qualities."

"I'm impressed with your knowledge of edible plants and things, Thomas," Jacob said surprisingly.

"Well, again," said Thomas, "we were trained and put in the wilderness for two months and told to survive on only what we found out there. We made animal traps, but mostly survived on plants, insects, grubs and other edibles we found."

"Sounds kind of disgusting to put you kids through that," Jacob said with a wrinkled-up nose.

"Survival, Jacob. If we went to battle, regular food wouldn't be there. We had to survive on our own with what was around us," Thomas said. "Don't get me wrong, we all lost a lot of weight out there, but we survived."

Jacob could see that this boy, like many others from his time, was well trained to cope with whatever came across his path. Jacob thought of himself as a great hiker, backpacker and explorer. He soon realized he was nothing compared to this cadet that was a true survivalist. Thomas would run Jacob into the ground if it came to who would live or die in the wilderness. To Jacob, the answer was easy. Thomas would be dragging Jacob's body out of the woods. Or worse yet, eating him after he died.

The two of them talked about survival techniques a while longer when Jacob realized the sun was soon to rise over the mountain. It seems that the short night visit was spent with casual conversation instead of trying to get to the bottom of Thomas's ordeal.

"I'm so sorry, Thomas," said Jacob. "We've talked the whole time about plants and trees and never talked about you."

Thomas looked at Jacob and said, "Look at it this way. If *you* don't survive out here, then I have no one to talk to and I'll never find out what my mission is supposed to be. I'll be stuck in these mountains forever. I needed to help you, so you can help me."

Jacob realized Thomas was right on with his explanation.

"We need you to survive, Jacob," Thomas said sternly. "Not just you, or not just me. We."

"Remember the things I told you," said Thomas. "And you'll be fine."

Thomas turned, walked into the pines and disappeared. Jacob, still somewhat exhausted from the whole night's excitement, crawled back into his tent and played back everything that happened over the last few hours. He knew he had a trying day ahead to find the Trail again and soon fell into a deep sleep.

Chapter Nine

Jacob continued to dream during his deep slumber. Once again, he dreamed he could feel the warm sun against his cheek. The thought of the bear next to his face entered his altered state and suddenly jarred his sleep into a rude awakening. He opened his eyes, thinking the bear was next to him, but this time found the warm, morning sun penetrating through the tent wall onto his cheek. No bear. A huge sigh of relief came over him and he realized he needed to start packing up his gear and go back to finding the Trail. He tightly rolled up his sleeping bag and sleeping pad and took them outside to secure them on his backpack. Jacob saw the mangled food pack and empty pouches scattered everywhere around his campsite. That's when reality set in…he had no food. He remembered what Thomas had told him last night about finding cattails. The only way to find them was to be near marshy lowlands. His goal was to climb the mountain over the other side to find the main Trail. Going back down the mountain he just climbed partway up wasn't in his plan. Jacob knew that there were no marshes on the mountainside, and if he continued his climb, he may not find anything at all, including the Trail. If that happened, he would surely be in a lot of serious trouble, not to mention not making it out at all. Jacob again remembered what Thomas told him… "We need you to survive. Not just you, or not just me. We." His survival wasn't just to make it out and survive for himself, it was for Thomas, too. Thomas needed him to live to get his answers. Jacob nodded his head and said to himself, "Okay, Thomas," because he understood what needed to be done. He packed up his tent, strapped everything on the backpack and threw it over his shoulders. He looked up towards the mountaintop, smiled and said, "Not yet," then headed back down the mountain to follow the river, hoping to find a marshy area with cattails.

Hiking down the mountain was much easier than hiking up, until he finally came to the river. Huge rocks and boulders were lining the riverbank and up to twenty yards up the slope, so walking alongside following the rushing water was ridiculously difficult. He found an area close to the water where he could replenish his water supply and he used his water filter to pump and purify the river water into his water bottles. He took a drink of the clear, cool water from his bottle, then another, and another, until the quart bottle was empty. He then pumped the bottle full with more river water, packed it up and continued downriver across the rocky terrain.

Hours passed and Jacob could feel himself getting pretty hungry. He still hadn't come across a marsh or pond to look for cattails, so he decided to grab some pine needles off a nearby pine tree to make some of that pine tea that Thomas mentioned. The fresh, stripped needles gave off a tremendous pine scent in his hand and just the aroma made him feel better. After a little maneuvering over the rocks, he found a flat area on a huge boulder where he could set up his little camp stove to boil some water. Jacob dug into his pack and found the stove, set it up on the flat area and lit it. Then he poured some water in a small pot, added the fresh pine needles, and brought it all to a boil. He boiled the needles and water a few minutes to get the pine nutrients and aroma into the water, then removed the small pot to cool down. The whole area wafted with the fragrance of fresh pine, as if Jacob just cleaned his house with a pine-scented spray. He poured a cupful into his tin cup, keeping the needles in the pot and then he took a sip. It didn't have the strong taste like a tea bag in hot water, but it definitely was a pine-tasting, hot drink. No color, just hot, clear, pine water. Jacob welcomed the fresh-tasting hot liquid and couldn't believe what just a handful of pine needles could do in hot water. He felt like Daniel Boone blazing the Boone Trail and surviving only on what was available in the woods. He thought to himself, "If only I had a long rifle to shoot game, I could just live out here forever." But he quickly realized what a softy he was and knew he couldn't shoot a precious animal. Eating plants, nuts and berries is one thing; eating an animal you shot in the woods is another. Jacob was by no means a vegetarian; he ate chicken, beef, pork and fish. However, shooting your own animal, watching it die, gutting it and butchering it in the woods? Jacob didn't have it in him to do that. He would probably die first.

The pine tea was completely satisfying to him. In fact, he poured the remaining water from the pot into his cup. Picking out the pine needles, he drank the rest of the warm liquid. It really was remarkable how much better he felt. It was like he had a little time to recharge his batteries and the pine tea gave him some energy. Plus, it actually was healthy for him. He was still hungry, but he did feel better and it was time to move on. Jacob packed his now-cool stove back into his pack and continued following the river downstream, climbing and hopping from boulder to boulder in hopes of some kind of food that would come across his path.

It wasn't too long before Jacob saw a clearing ahead that the river flowed into. It wasn't too large, but it looked like a marsh or pond. When he finally cleared the trees, he saw a small body of water with the river continuing to flow out at the opposite side. The pond was somewhat scummy with duckweed covering most of the water. Jacob panned the entire pond, no cattails in sight.

"Dammit," he whispered to himself. "This is not good."

He checked his compass heading, and then looked at his map. After hours of traveling down the river's edge, he actually was now farther away from the main Trail than he was before he left earlier this morning.

"Crap, that can't be," he said aloud. "This was supposed to be a fun trip. Not a death sentence." He had no choice. He moved on around the pond to follow the river.

The terrain had flattened considerably and walking became much easier along the riverbank. Jacob heard some splashing noises up ahead and could see there was another pond. When he approached, he saw a pair of beavers swimming and flapping their tails on the water. He immediately went back in time to when he, Annie and Jimmy were camping and Jimmy saw the beavers doing the exact same thing. Jacob lowered his backpack and sat down on a nearby rock near the water's edge. He watched the beavers just as Jimmy did, fascinated and mesmerized. Thoughts of Jimmy raced through his mind, quickly overtaking his emotions until he lowered his head and broke down in tears. Reality soon set back in when he realized he wasn't camping in Michigan with his family, he was lost in the Appalachian Mountains. He sat there, thinking to himself, "What the heck does a beaver eat?"

Jacob knew there had to be something in this

pond to keep the beavers alive. More than just algae or weeds. There had to be fish.

He picked up his pack and walked along the pond's edge, looking for any signs of fish, big or small. As he rounded a point of land that jutted into the water, he saw something and yelled aloud, "Fucking cattails!"

A small bed of green, healthy cattails were sprouting out of the water about four feet high. Jacob briskly walked over to the area and dropped his pack on the shore. He then took off his boots and socks and waded into the mucky water to the cattail bed. Knee deep in water and mud, he excitedly pulled on a cattail stem near the water's edge. It was firmly planted in the muck and made a suction sound as he extracted it from the pond. Jacob rinsed it off and looked at it curiously, with a smile.

"So, you really can eat these?" he said to the forest in amazement.

Suddenly, something brushed against his lower leg in the water. He was immediately startled, but didn't move for fear it was a copperhead, or something else poisonous he didn't know about. He looked down into the murky water, but couldn't see anything. He didn't move. Again, he felt something swish by his leg and even saw the water move on the surface. Something was down there and he couldn't see what it was. His heart was racing. He was trying to decide, "Should I continue to stand still until the water clears and then move away? Or should I just run like hell?" He thought if he made a sudden move to run, he might be bitten by whatever it was. Moreover, if it was a copperhead, that was serious trouble way out here. No doctor in sight. Not a good scenario. He had to stand still until the water cleared to see what was there.

It took about ten minutes for the stirred-up silt to settle enough to see into the water. Jacob looked around his feet, but saw nothing there.

"Where the hell did it go?" he thought to himself.

He looked around behind him, to each side and in front. Something jiggled the water to his left, in the cattails, that caught his attention. He looked on, motionless, searching for the snake's head to pop up out of the water. Jacob could see something dark below the surface of the water, but couldn't make out what it was. The water jiggled again. It came closer. Jacob was having trouble breathing at a normal rate. He was getting very nervous at what was going to materialize near his feet. It was now about three feet away and he could finally see what it was. It wasn't a copperhead snake…it was a catfish.

"Catfish!" Jacob exclaimed to himself quietly. "I need to catch him. Meat and vegetables!" he thought.

He slowly laid the cattail into the water, but stood perfectly still as to not startle his proposed meal. The catfish approached slowly, scavenging food off the bottom of the pond. He was oblivious to Jacob's presence. Now Jacob could see the fish was about a foot long, a sizable meal that would satisfy him and give him some strength to continue on his journey to the Trail.

Jacob slowly, and cautiously, stooped over with his hands, ready to try to grab the fish when he got close. He knew he'd have one shot at this and the odds were greatly against him catching a fish with his bare hands.

"If anyone is out there," he whispered to himself, "God…Thomas…Daniel Boone…I need your help."

The catfish was now at Jacob's feet. It sat motionless. Jacob had one attempt to make this happen. He had to plunge his hands into the water, grab the fish tightly, and carry it up on shore. Okay, here goes. He stared at the catfish; it was in a good position to make his move. Jacob's hands lunged into the water as if they had a mind of their own. He grabbed the fish and raised his hands up out of the water, the fish wiggling frantically within his grasp.

"I got it!" Jacob exclaimed. The catfish was slimy and slippery and he soon lost his grip. The fish wiggled out of his hands and started to fall to the water. Jacob, out of instinct, realized his meal was about to disappear and kicked at the fish before it hit the water. The catfish flew through the air to the shore like a punted football. Jacob ran to the fish and threw him farther up on the land so he wouldn't flop back into the water.

"Woohoo!" he exclaimed loudly. The beavers, hearing that scream, ducked down deep into their water home out of fear. Jacob looked proudly at his catch and said, "Thank you, God. Or Thomas. Or Daniel. Or everyone." He chuckled and went back into the mucky water and grabbed his cattail.

"This should be a good meal today," he said. He walked back to the shore and decided to make a campfire to cook his fish and vegetable.

Jacob gathered the wood and made a small fire pit. He then started the fire and got it going good enough to leave for a bit to clean his fish. After digging an elongated hole and placing a flat piece of wood in the bottom, just like he showed Jimmy, he laid the fish on the wood and sliced it open, cleaning out all the unwanted organs and blood. Then he took the fish to the water's edge and rinsed it thoroughly to get ready for cooking on the fire. Jacob found some large lily pad leaves and wrapped the fish in them to lay on the hot coals in the fire pit. The damp leaves kept the fish from burning on the direct fire, more like steaming the fish in a wrapped cocoon. The fire was now ready for cooking, so he placed the wrapped fish on the coals. Then he went and buried the hole with all the fish remains, returned to the fire and started slicing up the cattail into pieces that would fit into his pot. He remembered that Thomas told him he could boil out some of the bitter starch before eating and it would be easier on his stomach. Filling the pot with water and sliced cattails, he set the pot on the coals and waited for things to cook.

It took the fish and cattails about forty-five minutes to cook, so Jacob had time to sit and gaze out at the pond and tend the fire. He constantly flipped the leaf-wrapped fish to keep the leaves from burning too much. While sitting there, he noticed the beavers were back on top and swimming across the pond gathering sticks to repair their hut. Just like little carpenters, they'd place the stick or branch in the right spot and pack it down with mud to secure it. When they were satisfied with what they saw, they'd return to the water and retrieve another stick. If it wasn't the hut they were working on, it was the dam they built to make the pond. They were not only carpenters, they were designers and engineers. Jacob could definitely see why hard-working people were called busy beavers. They worked constantly until the task was completed.

By now, the cattails had been boiling a while and Jacob decided to remove them from the fire to cool down. The water was cloudy and bubbly with a starchy, coated film floating on top. He dumped off the water, rinsed them with clean water and set them aside to cool. About ten more minutes passed before he decided to pull the fish off the coals. He grabbed two sticks to grasp the fish package, dragged it off the fire and set it aside to cool also. Jacob reached into the pot next to him and pulled out a piece of the cattail. It was part of the lower rootstalk, white in color and cooked until soft. It looked like a leek or turnip. He sniffed it. It smelled a little like dirty mud, but it was clean.

"Okay, well, this is a first for me," he whispered. He popped the bite-sized morsel into his mouth and bit down with great anticipation at having some good, healthy, natural food.

"Ugh!" he yelled as he spit it out violently. "Are you fucking kidding me? Even the catfish weren't eating this shit!"

It tasted like a mucky, scummy pond bottom. After all, that's what it was growing in. Smelly muck. Years of soaked, rotted tree leaves laying on the bottom of the pond. Not fresh topsoil like your home garden. But Jacob knew that Thomas told him it was very healthy and would get him through until he found food to replenish his pack. He looked at the pot again with a wrinkled-up nose. He took another piece and slowly put it in his mouth. He cursed with every chomp he made. It was chewy, it was still bitter, and it tasted like a sewer. One after another, he continued to eat the cattail until most of the pot was gone, pinching his nose the whole time so he couldn't get much taste. But the wrenching, disgusting, shit-tasting swamp stick still made its way to his taste buds. After forcing most of the bitter stalk down, he turned to the catfish. He unwrapped the fish carefully with anticipation. The fish was steaming with heat, fully cooked and flakey. Jacob pulled off a bite-sized piece of the fleshy meat and put it in his mouth.

"Oh…my…God…" he exclaimed. "This is the best fish I have ever eaten!"

The tasty aquatic creature quickly extinguished the foul taste of the cattail root, making Jacob feel much better about his meal than he did a few minutes earlier. He continued to eat until there were only bones left on the leaves. He was full. He was content. And he was alive.

By this time, most of the day had passed and the deep valley was turning from bright sunlight into subdued darkness. It was by no means too dark to see, but it definitely was too dark to travel on. Jacob knew a second night in the wilderness was imminent.

He gathered more firewood to carry him through the night and set up his tent. Tonight would definitely be a little chillier than last night because he was now in the valley and next to water. Dampness set in quickly and a chill rapidly came over the air. Jacob threw some large logs on the fire to stoke it up and throw some heat, then put on a sweatshirt to keep warm. He sat back and thought of the past events of the last day or so and how lucky he's been. Somebody seemed to be watching out for his safety so he could continue on, with not only *his* quest, but Thomas's, too. He could've been bitten by a copperhead snake, he wasn't. He could've been swept far down a raging river and drowned, he didn't. He could've been eaten or mauled by a huge black bear, he wasn't. And he could've starved after his food was gone, but through Thomas's training, he found food. Yes, someone was watching over him.

As the darkness set in, he sat there listening to the frogs croaking in the pond and wondered if this was a safe place to be for the night. Not that he had much choice, but the bears were plentiful in the Appalachians and he knew that first hand. If he was being helped along the way to survive, that was great. But what if it was just dumb luck? He couldn't help but think he may not be so lucky the next time.

The night air was still and there was no breeze down in the valley. No leaves rustled and a misty fog set in over the pond and low areas. Jacob threw a couple more good-sized logs on the fire and climbed into his shelter. He knew Thomas would arrive later and wanted to get some sleep before he came by. He was almost asleep before his head hit the small pillow.

About midnight, Jacob was awakened. Not from noise, from silence. The frogs ceased croaking and crickets were hushed. He laid there and listened. He could hear multiple footsteps running around the shore and campsite. Whatever was out there, they were searching for food. It almost sounded like they were hyper and frantic out there, constantly running back and forth and making little yipping sounds. Jacob recognized these sounds from camping with Annie and Jimmy. They were coyotes. They hunt in packs. He knew there had to be quite a few of them out there. He could hear them digging and ripping apart an old, half-rotted tree log on the ground. Jacob quietly reached into his pack and pulled out a gift that Annie gave him for one of his birthdays…a night vision scope. These make it possible to see into the dark night with infrared light and make it look like daylight through the scope without projecting any visible light. You can see everything clearly within a hundred yards. But Jacob didn't need to see a hundred yards, he only needed to see about forty feet. He slowly, and quietly, unzipped the flap covering his window, just enough to see out of the tent. The coyotes were too busy digging and carrying on to even notice him nearby. He pushed the button on the scope to activate the night vision and slowly raised it to his eyes.

"Oh my God," he whispered silently to himself. There were six coyotes, all digging frantically at the semi-rotted, hollow log. Something was obviously in that log that they wanted. Grubs? Maybe a field mouse or squirrel? Jacob continued to watch. One of the coyotes finally ripped a hole in the log big enough to get his nose in there. The rest of the wild dogs starting whimpering and carrying on in excitement. Now, all Jacob could see of the one coyote was his body, because his whole head was inside the log trying to pull something out. Finally, after a few minutes more, the coyote withdrew from the log with a terrified, wiggling rabbit in its mouth. He ran off into the woods and all the coyotes followed, barking, yelping loudly and carrying on as if they were celebrating a great accomplishment. Jacob watched through the scope when they stopped about thirty yards into the trees. He could see them rip the rabbit apart into pieces, the rabbit still wiggling, until moments later, it was still. He could only imagine the terror that rabbit went through, knowing he was trapped in the log and being hunted down by savages that only wanted to eat him. The thought of being caught and ripped apart alive brought sadness to Jacob, but he also knew that this was the cycle of life for these animals. Some live to old age, some never make it much farther than birth. It's just the way it works out here. He also realized that if he was visited by a black bear, or two, he would be the rabbit. It was not a good feeling to have.

Ten minutes later, the frogs started croaking again and the crickets began their tireless chirps. The coyotes had their temporary morsels and moved on. Jacob slumped back into his sleeping bag and thanked God that he was still alive and okay. He soon fell back asleep listening to the mixed serenade of the forest symphony.

Jacob awoke at 2:30am because of a sour stomach and cramps. He knew it had to be from all that raunchy cattail crap he ate. He didn't feel like vomiting, but he did feel nauseous. He unzipped his tent door and crawled outside. The fire was nothing but glowing embers glistening in the darkness and the moon was shining through the trees, casting an eerie glow in the fog on the pond. The night air was damp and chilly, so Jacob walked to the magenta glow and threw on a couple of small logs to get the fire going again. He sat back for a moment and knew Thomas would be coming soon, then tossed a couple of larger logs on. The fire rose up out of the pit with a crackle and instantly lit up the camp area. His stomach felt a little queasy, so he thought that maybe making some of that great pine tea would help soothe his misery. He stripped off a handful of pine needles from a nearby tree and prepared everything for his drink. As he sat there waiting for his pot to boil with the pine needles inside, he listened to the night sounds around him. Frogs croaked, crickets carried on with their chirps and two owls were hooting to each other far off in the woods. He couldn't help but smile and knew that this was really God's country, a place that was slowly diminishing around the world because of production and expansion. The best part, he thought, was that places like this were government-protected areas and they would never change. People would always have a wilderness somewhere to enjoy and explore. That was so important not only for human enjoyment, but for the animals and environment as well.

The water was now boiling with the scent of pine everywhere. Jacob removed the pot from the heat and poured the tea into his cup. Steam rose and he blew on the liquid a little to help cool it down before drinking. He took a sip.

"That is just so fucking amazing," he said aloud. "Pine needles and water. Who'd a thought?"

He continued to drink until it was time to refill. His stomach was actually feeling a little better and he knew Thomas, though just a young teenager, was taught well for survival. He poured the rest of the tea in his cup and sat back, waiting for Thomas's arrival.

A few minutes had passed before Thomas approached the campsite from the foggy trees. Jacob looked at his watch…it was 3:40am.

"Right on time, Thomas," he said with a smile as he stood up.

"Did you expect anything less?" Thomas said surprisingly.

"Well, no…I guess not," replied Jacob a little sheepishly.

Thomas looked around and commented, "I see you're not back on the Trail yet. I didn't think I'd find you farther away than you were last night. What happened?"

"Ummm…I got nervous I wouldn't find any

cattails if I continued on up the mountain, and I was really hungry in the morning, so I decided to go back down and follow the river until I found some," Jacob replied. "I ended up here," he looked down at his feet, embarrassed, "farther away."

"And did you find some?" asked Thomas.

"Yes, finally," said Jacob wrinkling up his nose. "I sliced one up and boiled it, like you said, to get the starchy bitterness out. It was still bitter, but I ate it anyway."

Thomas smiled with surprise and said, "Good for you, Jacob! How do you feel?"

"I have a sour stomach, but the pine tea is helping," Jacob replied. "You know, that bullshit cattail tasted like shit. I mean, really, shit."

Thomas laughed and said, "I didn't say it tasted good, I said it would help you survive."

Jacob looked at Thomas and yelled, "It tasted so bad I *wanted* to die!"

Thomas laughed hysterically. "You're alive, Jacob. Be thankful for that."

"You know what I'm thankful for? I'm thankful I caught that catfish and had a great meal with that disgusting, swamp water, foul-tasting weed," exclaimed Jacob.

"Catfish?" asked Thomas. "You had a catfish?"

"Yes, I did," Jacob said proudly. "Caught it with my bare hands and threw it up on the shore."

"Your bare hands?"

"Well, kind of," said Jacob. "I had him in my hands until the slippery devil slipped out. Then I kicked him as he was falling and he flew through the air like a kicked ball, landed on the sandy bank."

Thomas laughed again and said, "I wish I was here to see that one."

"It made my whole meal complete," said Jacob.

Thomas paused a moment, then asked, "I'm just curious, Jacob. If you ate a whole catfish, why did you eat the cattail?"

Jacob looked at him a bit confused, then said, "Because you said I need those to survive."

"Well, that's true. You do need those…if there's nothing else to eat," replied Thomas. "But you had a whole catfish. You really didn't need the cattail at all."

"CHRIST, THOMAS!" Jacob yelled.

"Again, it's Thomas Garland Jefferson, not Christ Thomas," he said laughing.

"You didn't tell me I didn't need to eat those

fucking cattails if I found something else to eat," Jacob said loudly.

Thomas was still laughing when he replied, "I didn't think you'd find anything else. Let alone catch a fish with your bare hands. And, uh… foot."

Jacob laughed, "I wish there was a video of that one."

Thomas looked puzzled and asked, "What's a video?"

"Oh, never mind," Jacob said. "It's not important. Come…sit by the fire while I puke and shit out all of this delicious cattail gourmet I had."

The two of them chuckled, sat down and stared into the fire.

"We didn't get a chance to talk last night about you, Thomas," said Jacob.

"There were more important things to discuss then," replied Thomas. "We can talk about whatever you want now."

"I want to talk about you," Jacob said with a concerned voice.

"Okay. Well, I still have that feeling of following you to get answers."

"That's good, Thomas," Jacob said. "I want to

find those answers. What else can you tell me right now that might help me figure this out?"

"I still have a few friends from the battle that are walking with me," he said. "The little boy is showing up more."

"Why do you think this boy is following you?" asked Jacob. "Did he get injured or die in the battle with you and your friends?"

"I don't remember him there. He wasn't in the field with us; maybe he was in the town or something?" Thomas asked.

Jacob looked at Thomas and asked, "Does he ever say anything to you? Has he spoken to anyone else that's with you?"

Thomas shook his head no.

"I've never heard him talk to anyone. Not yet anyway."

"Maybe he's looking for answers, too. He might think you'll find them for him," Jacob said.

Thomas had a look of confusion on his face.

"He doesn't look like he's searching like I am," said Thomas. "He just walks around, following me wherever I go and then vanishes. It's like he's patiently waiting for something to happen. The right time, you know?"

"Maybe," Jacob replied. "Or maybe he just likes you and feels comfortable being near you."

"Don't get me wrong, I don't mind him coming around," Thomas said. "I mean, he's a cute kid and all. Just seems like he's waiting for something, instead of looking for something."

Jacob looked at Thomas and spoke with a voice of deep concern, "I think he feels safe being around you. You have something he needs. I wouldn't discourage him at all, Thomas. He may have an answer we're looking for."

"Like I said, I don't mind him being around. I actually enjoy his company, even though he hasn't talked to me."

Jacob looked a little puzzled, but still asked the question, "When do you see him the most?"

Thomas answered quickly. "Whenever I'm on my way to see you. Then, just before I get to wherever you are, he disappears."

"That's really strange," Jacob said. "Do you think he's looking for an answer from me?"

"I don't know, sir. He doesn't talk to me, so I don't have an answer for that."

"Did he follow you here tonight?" Jacob asked inquisitively.

"Of course," Thomas replied. "But, he was gone before I made it around the pond."

Jacob was now more confused than Thomas. Why was this little boy following Thomas, and why did he always leave before Thomas got to Jacob? What's more, why did Thomas think the boy was waiting for something, possibly the right moment for something to happen before revealing why he was even there? Too many questions and not enough answers, Jacob thought.

The two of them talked on for another hour before the morning sun was starting to illuminate the horizon over the mountain. Birds started chirping and little chipmunks were beginning to emerge and frolic in the grass and leaves. Thomas stood to his feet and said, "It's time for me to go."

"I know, Thomas. Today I'm finding the Trail again," Jacob said with a positive attitude.

"It's a long way off, but you can do it," said Thomas. "You're a survivor now."

Jacob looked at Thomas with sincerity, "Thank you, Thomas. That means a lot coming from you."

"Just don't forget to grab some cattails before you go," Thomas said while chuckling. "Seriously, you won't run into much of anything on the way back up the mountain. Put some in your pack just in case."

Jacob cringed at the thought of having to eat that vile food source again. He knew Thomas was right, but hoped he'd find something else along the way.

"See you later," Thomas said. "Be careful."

"I will, thanks. Later, dude," replied Jacob.

Thomas looked at Jacob, confused again and said, "I'm sorry? Did you say dude? What's a dude?"

"Never mind," Jacob said laughing. "It's a modern-day expression for friend."

Oh," Thomas said. "Okay, see you later…dude."

They both laughed, Thomas turned and walked into the mist. He was gone. Jacob needed just a short couple of hours to sleep before packing up and starting his long trek back to the trail. He crawled into the tent and plopped down for his restful nap.

Chapter Ten

Jacob felt quite rested after he awoke two hours later. He packed up his gear, folded his tent and strapped it all to the backpack. Then he looked out at the quiet pond, focusing his sight on the cattails. He said to himself, "Really? I have to grab a couple of those vile weeds and bring them in case I need more food on the way?" He gagged at the thought of eating those again. But he knew Thomas was right, waded into the water and grabbed a couple of juicy looking, tender stalks that smelled like sewage when he extracted them from the muck. Rinsing them off, they went into his pack and he was once again on his way in search of the main Trail.

Jacob knew the Trail was well over the high ridge that was directly in front of him, so he left the river valley and started his long, arduous climb up the mountain. Once again, there were no trails to follow. He had only his compass and map to get him where he needed to go.

Up the slope, around the boulders and in-between the downed trees he climbed. He had to take numerous breaks because of the tremendous amount of exertion involved and he tired easily. It really made him feel his fifty-years of age instead of his thirties when he hiked before with Annie and Jimmy. He often spoke to them on his breaks, wishing they were here with him and having fun together. He knew it would've been a fantastic family trip.

It was about 2pm before Jacob realized he couldn't take the hunger anymore. All this hiking, climbing and traversing used up a lot of his energy and he needed something to replenish that. There were plenty of pine trees with needles to make his tea, but he needed something more substantial in his stomach. He happened across some large oak trees and found numerous acorns laying on the ground. But most were laying there from last year and were rotted and soft. The new crop hadn't materialized yet, so fresh acorns were not on the menu. He set down his pack and took a seat on a nearby stump. Exhausted and weak, he knew what he had to do. He had to cook and eat those muck smelling, shit tasting, disgusting swamp weeds Thomas called food. He suddenly had a brilliant idea…how about cooking the pine needles in the same pot *with* the cattails? Maybe the pine would mask the cattail taste and make it much more enjoyable to eat, also giving him the energy he needed from the pine tea, all wrapped up in one package. Excitedly, he filled a pot with some water, cut up the cattails and threw in a good handful of pine needles. Then he started his camp stove, set the pot of improvised soon-to-be, gourmet, vegetable soup on the flame and waited for it to boil. When the water began to churn and roll, he lowered the heat and simmered the pot for about ten more minutes. The cattails became soft, the starch boiled out and the entire area had the aroma of fresh pine. Jacob removed the pot from the fire and set it aside. His stomach was growling with hunger and his taste buds were salivating with anticipation of a great tasting meal. After cooling a bit, Jacob skimmed off the starchy residue on top of the water and popped a fresh, pine-smelling morsel right into his mouth, ready to chomp down on his succulent vegetable. And chomp down he did.

"OH DEAR GOD!" he shouted. "It tastes like little pine-coated shit logs!" Yes, it was disgusting. But Jacob knew he had to eat it. All of it. As foul tasting as it was, it had to end up in his stomach to do any good. He continued to stare at each piece and eat, slowly, gagging with a couple of dry heaves, until every piece was consumed.

"There. I did it," he said to himself aloud. "Now I just hope I can keep it down." He made another small pot of fresh pine tea and drank that down, hoping to kill the raunchy taste of the mucky pond in his mouth, but it didn't help. It was as if the scummy water was burned into his taste buds. Jacob then threw his gear together and continued up the mountain, still searching for that damn main Trail.

It was close to 5pm before he reached the summit and started down the other side. According to his map, he was getting real close to the main Trail again. He continued down the slope a few hundred yards until he came perpendicular to a well-marked path. It was the Appalachian Trail. He was so overjoyed that he wanted to bend down and kiss the dirt, but he figured he already had enough foul taste in his mouth from his gourmet lunch. The map showed a family campground only a few miles down the Trail and he knew he could replenish his food supply and probably just camp there for the night, getting the much-needed rest his body craved. He also knew that it would probably be too busy for Thomas to show, but he knew Thomas would understand his situation and still return the next night. Thomas was not about to leave him without the answers he was looking for.

Jacob slowly staggered into the campground a couple of hours later and found a picnic table to drop his pack onto and sit down. He was exhausted from bushwhacking and climbing mountains the past two days, let alone eating disgusting cattails instead of having a real meal. He rested his head on his pack and quickly dozed off.

He fell into a deep sleep and dreamed about Annie. He could see them enjoying camping together, even hear her voice saying, "Jacob. Jacob."

In his dream, she was nudging him and kept calling, "Jacob."

Finally, he jerked awake and saw a woman standing next to him, shaking his arm and saying, "Jacob!"

It was Diane and Parker. Shiloh came running over and slobbered all over his face. Jacob was now definitely awake.

"Oh….well, hello guys!" Jacob said surprisingly.

Diane smiled and said, "Hi there! You were really sound asleep there."

"I must've dozed off," he said. "I've had an exhausting couple of days."

"What the hell happened, Jake?" Parker asked. "Oops…sorry. I mean Jacob."

Jacob frowned at Parker. "I took a wrong turn on the Trail and got lost. By the time I realized it, I was too far away to turn back and didn't want to lose more time, so I bushwhacked through the wilderness."

"Oh, Jacob," Diane said softly. "You really look awful. Are you okay?"

"Well, my first night out I was visited by a black bear that ate everything I had," he said. "I had to forage in the wild to survive."

"Well, it's a good thing you know what to eat and what not to eat out there. There's a lot of plants and things that will kill you, man. Dead, you know?" replied Parker.

"Yes, I know," said Jacob. "Truthfully, I think I'd

rather die next time than eat those disgusting cattails."

"Disgusting?" asked Diane. "They're excellent! And a great food source. They're everywhere you find a pond."

Jacob looked at her as if she was out of her mind. Excellent, she says? What drugs was she on?

"They tasted like a goddamn sewer!" Jacob yelled. "I can still taste those mucky weeds in my mouth. How the hell can you even think that they're excellent?"

"You did cut off the lower eight to ten inches of the stalk before you ate them, right?" asked Diane.

"What? Cut off what?" Jacob asked surprisingly.

Parker let out a huge roar of laughter. Diane immediately followed.

"Oh, Jacob," she said with sincerity. "The lower part of the cattail, the part that grows in the mucky bottom...that's the part you cut off before you eat it. The rest of the stalk basically has no taste at all and it's wonderful. No wonder you hated them."

Jacob stared at them, mouth wide open with shock. All this time he could've had a great meal of tender cattails, but instead he gagged on musty, mucky stalks of shitty cattail growth that he was supposed to discard before eating. He thought for a moment, and then whispered, "Thomas."

"Did you say Thomas?" asked Diane. "Who's Thomas?"

"Oh, he's the one that told me about the cattails originally. I guess he neglected to tell me about cutting off the root," Jacob said, thinking to himself that a young, Confederate ghost set him up.

Parker was still laughing pretty hard. "Nice friends you have, Jacob."

Diane, not laughing anymore, looked at Jacob and said, "Stay the night here tonight. Have dinner with us. I'll cook up a great meal. You can stock up on your food at the General Store in the morning."

Jacob, of course, didn't want to impose, but could not turn down this great offer. "I would love that. Thank you."

Parker grabbed Jacob's backpack and flung it over his shoulder.

"Let's go, gang," he said.

They proceeded to walk through the campground until coming to Diane and Parker's site. And Shiloh's, too.

"Here we go, man," Parker, pointed. "You can

set up your tent right there. There's plenty of room here."

"Thanks," said Jacob appreciatively. "That'll work great."

While Jacob unpacked his tent and gear, Diane disappeared and walked over to the General Store to get things for a great dinner. She returned about twenty minutes later, carrying a couple of sacks of food…and three bottles of wine.

"I think you're going to like this dinner, Jacob," Diane said excitedly.

Jacob saw the wine and asked, "Is that cooking wine you have?"

Diane and Parker both laughed when Parker said, "Cooking wine? We're in the woods, man, not on a TV cooking show. This is for our soothing pleasure."

Jacob smiled. "I'm down. I am so down," he said laughing. "I'm so far down that I have to reach up to touch bottom."

They all laughed when Parker had to join in and say, "I'm so far down that I need a parachute to jump off a dime!"

Diane looked at Jacob, rolling her eyes. Then Parker jumped in again, thinking this was a fun game, and said, "I'm so far down that I get a nosebleed when I stand up!"

Jacob looked at Diane and smiled. Parker immediately jumped in once more and said, "I'm so far down..."

"STOP IT, PARKER!" Diane yelled. "You're bringing us *all* down!"

Shiloh turned and walked away. Even the dog couldn't take it anymore.

"Now that that's over with," Diane said, "that store has so many things. They have wild game, too. Jacob, do you like possum and squirrel?"

Jacob had a subdued look of horror on his face. He was thinking that this great dinner was going to be burgers, or perhaps chicken or something. Not a possum...or squirrel. He suddenly thought that maybe the cattails really weren't that bad after all. Diane and Parker were staring at him, excitedly waiting for his response.

"Umm...I'm not really sure I can answer that," said Jacob with a quivering voice. "I've never eaten those before. Or thought that I would have to. I mean, have the opportunity to have them." He looked really uncomfortable at the thought of eating those nasty varmints. "Truthfully, I don't think it's something I want to try."

Diane and Parker stared at Jacob, as if they were insulted because he wouldn't try those delicious rodents. Then they busted out laughing.

"She's fucking with ya, man!" Parker yelled. "Who the fuck would eat that shit in a modern campground? They don't have that crap here!"

"We're having barbequed chicken legs, ribs, coleslaw and a macaroni salad, with cheesecake for dessert," Diane said smiling. "And top it off with wine."

Jacob breathed a sigh of relief. "Now, that's what I'm talking about!" he exclaimed.

"I'm down, too," said Parker.

"Don't even think about it, Parker. We know how down you are," said Diane.

Parker walked over to a nearby grill, all the campsites had them. He dumped in a bag of charcoal and lit the fire. Soon the coals were turning white hot, almost ready for the meat that Diane seasoned and prepared. Jacob felt helpless just sitting there watching, but Diane cracked open the first bottle of wine and that made things go a little easier. Parker cooked the meat and drank wine, Diane prepared the coleslaw and macaroni salad and drank wine, and Jacob sat there watching…and drank wine.

Time passed quickly and all the food was on the picnic table, ready to devour. A second bottle of wine was opened for dinner and they all dug in to have a great feast. Jacob couldn't wait to taste some real food again. His mouth was watering before the first bite even entered his body. He thought to himself as he stared at the table full of food, 'Should I have a chicken leg first? No, maybe some ribs. Wait, how about some of those delicious salads?'

It really didn't matter what order he ate the food in. He couldn't even remember where he started, he just knew that this was the best meal he'd had in a long time. There wasn't a whole lot of conversation going on because everyone was too busy eating, except when Jacob got caught slipping some meat to Shiloh under the table.

"You better stop feeding him, Jacob," Diane told him, "or he'll be sleeping with you in your tent tonight. He farts a lot when he eats our food."

Jacob looked shocked, "He farts?"

"Smells so bad it'll kill a rhino," said Parker. "And I thought mine were bad."

"They are," chimed Diane. "Seems like you two are always in competition with each other. I've even contemplated going to the Army Surplus store and buying a gas mask."

Jacob laughed. "Okay, I get your point. No more food for Shiloh. I don't need him to have to stay in my tent." Jacob looked at Diane and said, "But there's nothing I can do about Parker. You're on your own with that one."

All three pretty much devoured everything on the table. Jacob felt fabulous after that enormous feast and after cleaning up, they all sat at the table, drank wine and talked. Jacob told them of his ordeal of being lost, the near attack of a copperhead, falling into the river and being carried downstream, and, of course, the visiting friendly bear that ate everything in his food bag. They couldn't believe he went through so much in only a couple of days after seeing them. Luckily, he found his way back to the Trail that actually brought him to them for a great meal and companionship.

The campground had full amenities, including clean rest rooms and a building that housed private showers. Parker stood up and said, "Well, kiddies, I'm going to go hit the shower and soak a while to get this trail dust off me. Feel free to continue without my presence."

Diane looked at him with a smile and said, "I thought we'd just sit here in silence until you returned."

Parker looked at her, then Jacob, and whispered, "She's never been silent. Don't let her fool you, man."

Diane picked up the bar of soap on the table, threw it at him laughing, and said, "Go take your shower, poophead."

He grabbed the soap, towel and a change of clothes and off he went, laughing aloud.

Diane, now alone with Jacob, refilled the wine glasses, looked at him and asked, "Well, have you thought about what I said? You've had a lot of time to yourself over the past couple of days. Are you coming to terms with yourself?"

Jacob looked at her, took a large gulp of wine, and then returned his look. He was definitely feeling the effects of drinking wine the past couple of hours and felt he was ready to spill his guts to her.

"Diane, I feel comfortable talking with you," he said. "I think it's time you knew the whole story."

She reached across the table and cupped his

hand between both of hers with a soft, gentle touch and said, "I'm listening, Jacob."

"That night when we were at the shelter, you said you felt a spirit nearby and then it was gone," Jacob explained.

"Yes," she said. "I remember."

"Well, what you felt was real," said Jacob. "It was Thomas."

"Thomas?" she asked. "Wait; is that the same Thomas that told you about the cattails?"

"The same," he replied. "His name is Thomas Garland Jefferson. He's the grandson of President Thomas Jefferson."

Diane had a puzzled look on her face, but she knew Jacob was telling the truth. What reason would he have to make up a story like this?

"You've got that look on your face like I'm crazy or something," he said.

"No, I'm sorry Jacob, I don't mean to look like that at all," she said sincerely. "I believe you. I believe you because I sensed that spirit myself. Tell me how this is Thomas Jefferson's grandson. How did this all come about?"

"It actually started back when I originally hit the

Trail. He visited me at night, but I didn't know it was him until later," explained Jacob.

"Why is he making himself known to you?" she asked.

"Okay, let me tell you everything I know," he said. "I started hearing noises every night at 3:40am. One night a bear came into the camp, I could see him at the screen door of the shelter. Then something scared him and he ran off. When I looked at my watch, it was 3:40am. I looked outside and saw a figure near the fire pit, dressed in gray and covered with mud, but he wouldn't come in. I wanted to thank him, but instead he just walked away. Finally, after a couple more encounters at night, I was able to get him to trust me and come inside."

Diane asked, "Did you know he was a spirit then?"

"Not yet. He said he was at war and was dressed in gray. He looked like a Confederate soldier from the Civil War. In fact, I thought he was a re-enactor. When he sat down, he explained to me he was the grandson of Thomas Jefferson. I laughed and told him that was impossible because he would be over 150 years old. He got real serious and was offended that I didn't believe him, so I asked him if he hurt his head or something, thinking maybe he fell and had a concussion and wasn't thinking straight," Jacob replied.

"What did he say to that?"

"He said his head hurt, so I offered to take a closer look at it," said Jacob. "He agreed to let me examine him and as I went to brush his hair out of the way, my hand passed right through his head."

"And that's when you knew he was a spirit and not a real man," confirmed Diane.

"Yes," he replied. "Needless to say, I was shocked. I sat back down and asked him to tell me everything that happened.

Jacob continued to tell Diane everything he knew; that Thomas was a Cadet from VMI and all 257 cadets were given the order to charge at New Market, that he received a head wound trying to save his friend, that he died at 3:40am three days later in a field hospital from an infection he got in that muddy, manure, farm field, and that he felt compelled to follow Jacob, but didn't know why.

"That's why he comes at 3:40am, and that's why he came the night we were there, to talk to you again,"

Diane confirmed. "But he left because he knew you couldn't talk."

"Yes," Jacob said. "I also told him that there must be a reason why he hasn't moved on, like he has some sort of unfinished business to do before God accepts him into Heaven, or wherever he's supposed to be. I promised him I would help him find that reason."

"Just how do you think you're going to do that?" asked Diane.

"Right now, all I'm doing is meeting with him every night possible to talk things out," he said. "Maybe something will click and I can get him to finally move on into a peaceful dimension."

"Do you think you're getting closer to a solution?" Diane asked.

"I don't know," he said discouraged. "Now he's thrown another iron in the fire. He said a little boy shows up and travels with him, but then disappears before he gets to me."

Diane, looking puzzled, asked, "A little boy? How long has the little boy been in the picture?"

"He said he arrived just when he started following me," Jacob said. "But he doesn't stick around when Thomas meets me. Thomas thinks the boy might be waiting for the right time to make it known why he's here."

Shiloh walked over and set his head down on Jacob's lap, as if he understood the whole conversation and felt compassion for Jacob. Both he and Diane smiled at the gesture while Jacob petted Shiloh's head.

"This is quite an animal," Jacob said smiling.

"I think he's a rekindled spirit from someone, like a reincarnation," said Diane.

Jacob looked up and asked Diane a question. "What do *you* make of all this stuff with Thomas? What do *you* think I should do?"

Diane thought a moment, then looked him in the eyes and replied, "Thomas is looking for something. He's confused and wants to know why he's still here, wandering around. He was drawn to you. He feels you're the one person that can help him. You're the one, Jacob. You're the chosen one. You need to keep talking with him until the answer is known. You can do this. I can help you."

Jacob looked sorrowful thinking the task might be too big for him to handle, but he knew Diane was right. He needed to stick with it and keep Thomas's trust. And Diane offered to help.

"I'm not sure what you can do, Diane," Jacob said.

"Jacob, I'm a spirit sensitive person. I can feel the presence of a spirit. I can only do this because I'm compassionate and understand the spirit world. Most spirits that I come in contact with feel comfortable that I'm there, because they feel I relate to them and can communicate their needs."

"I just don't know if he'll accept you," replied Jacob concerned. "He might just shy away and not return."

"Jacob, if he doesn't show up here tonight, I promise you he'll come back again. He trusts you. He won't abandon you. If not tonight, maybe tomorrow night. Or, the next night. But he'll come back. If he sees that we're friends, he may open up to me and make himself known."

"I really hope you're right, Diane," Jacob said. "I need all the help I can get. This boy needs answers, that's why he's following me. I obviously have something he's looking for. Maybe that's why *our* paths crossed, I mean with you and Parker, because you can help me figure this out."

"We *will* figure this out, Jacob." She thought for a moment, and then spoke. "Here's what I'd like to do, if you don't mind," Diane explained. "You, Parker and I are all headed in the same direction down the Trail. How would you feel if we traveled together so we could meet Thomas and try to come to a solution?"

Jacob looked relieved, hoping that this idea of Diane's would work. "I'm all for it," he said excitedly. "I just hope Thomas is, too."

"I'm willing to try," she said. "Pray on it tonight, Jacob."

Just then, a whistling man came strolling towards them. It was Parker returning after his shower. "Now, I know you guys weren't silent while I was gone. Did I miss anything good?"

"Nothing that would interest you," Diane said.

"What's that supposed to mean?" asked Parker." I'm interested in everything."

"Everything?" Diane asked surprisingly. "Are you kidding me? You're interested in everything?"

"Of course," he said chuckling. "I'm a counselor at a school. I have to be open to everything that's out there."

"Okay," Diane said. "We talked about spirits and

ghosts."

"Except that," said Parker. "We don't have those in school, so it's an area I don't go into. Besides, you've got that covered."

Diane looked at Jacob and said, "He figures if I do that part, then he can have nothing to do with it. Spirits and ghosts spook him."

"Oh my God, what a great line!" Parker exclaimed. "Spirits and ghosts spook me. Sounds like a keeper to me!"

"Just don't tell us you're down with it, please," said Jacob.

They all started laughing; Diane poured the last bit of wine in all three glasses. "Jacob said he'd love to have company on the Trail and asked us to travel with him, if that's okay honey," Diane asked.

"Of course it's okay! It can get pretty lonely out there, especially if something goes wrong and there's nobody around to help," Parker said. "That's why we bring Shiloh; he usually scares things away before they even get close to us."

"Thanks guys, I really appreciate the company," Jacob said with heartfelt emotion. Shiloh jumped up on Jacob and licked his face repeatedly as if to show his approval of the whole idea, too. They finished drinking their wine when Jacob decided this was a good time to go take a shower himself. It was getting late and he wanted to rest before Thomas was due to arrive, even though that was questionable because of all the people in the campground. He thanked Diane and Parker for a great dinner, great wine and great company, then knelt down and hugged Shiloh for understanding, too. He headed off to the showers and afterwards, turned in for some rest before looking for Thomas.

The campground was quite noisy into the night with partiers drinking, laughing and carrying on. Jacob looked at his watch…it was 2:50am; he knew Thomas may be arriving shortly. He decided to get up, go sit on the picnic table, and wait. Diane and Parker's tent was dark and quiet and he knew they were asleep, so he tried not to make any noise. He also didn't want Shiloh to jump up while in their tent and startle them. Jacob sat quietly, looking around the campground into the tree line hoping to see a ghostly figure approach from within. He soon checked his watch again; it was 3:18. He knew Thomas could appear at any moment. The noisy campers were laughing and yelling, probably drunk on their asses and Jacob realized that this meeting was not going to happen. It was 3:40; no sign of Thomas. He sat there and waited until nearly 4am before silently creeping back into his tent for the remainder of the night, constantly playing back Diane's words of encouragement, 'I promise you he'll come back again. He trusts you. He won't abandon you.'

Feeling somewhat relieved with her words, he fell back asleep.

Jacob heard Diane and Parker outside rustling around, starting to clean up and pack things away. It was 7:45am when he exited his shelter and joined them.

"Good morning, sunshine!" exclaimed Parker.

"Yeah, yeah," replied Jacob. "I have a headache."

"We all do," replied Diane. "It's the sugar in the wine. It'll do that to you. Wine at night guarantees a headache in the morning."

Jacob looked confused, but didn't ask any questions. He just thought he'd let it ride. Diane handed a bottle of aspirin to Jacob.

"Here, take a couple," she said. "We already had ours."

Jacob grabbed the bottle and shook out two pills. He popped them in his mouth while Diane handed him a bottle of water.

"I'm making some bacon and eggs before we leave, Jacob. Are you interested?"

"Goddamn right I am!" he exclaimed. They chuckled while Diane got things ready to cook.

"I think I'll head over to the General Store and stock up on my food supply," Jacob said. "Need anything while I'm there?"

"We stocked our packs yesterday. Thanks for asking, though," Parker replied.

"Okay, see you guys in a bit," he said. Jacob walked through the campground over to the store, picking up beer bottles and cans that were strewn along the way, tossing them into the receptacles. He was greeted inside the store by a girl behind the counter, a pretty, blond in her early thirties with her long hair tied back in a ponytail. She was wearing a checkered shirt with denim overalls; the kind they make into short-shorts.

"Good morning, sir," she said with her Dolly Parton voice. "How can I help you?"

"Good morning. I just need to pick up some food

for my backpack," he said. Jacob browsed around, picking up snacks, freeze-dried pouches of food, a block of cheese, a skinny loaf of French bread, some granola for breakfast and packets of coffee and tea.

He walked back to the counter with an awkward armful of items, dropping most of them along the way and setting them down for checkout. He walked back and retrieved the items he dropped.

"There, that should about do it," he said.

"You do know that we have little baskets at the door for you to put your items in when you shop?" she said jokingly.

"I really didn't notice. I was too busy being mesmerized by your beauty," he said smiling.

"Look at you, sweet talker!" she said looking him up and down. "I can tell you're a charmer with the ladies. You are staying another night, aren't you? We could have some fun," she asked inquisitively.

Normally, Jacob would have no plans or timetable to adhere to and he knew this sexy, little cashier was hitting on him, offering what seemed to be a memorable night. But unfortunately, he did have plans and people to travel with, so he was extremely disappointed at having to decline this unbelievable offer.

"I'm sorry, sweetheart, but I have people I'm traveling with. They wouldn't understand if I told them I wanted to stay another night, and then not spend it with them."

"Too bad," she said. "It would've been a great stress reliever from hiking that Trail."

Jacob just stared at her in amazement. She kept ringing up his groceries until he finally got out the words, "Honey, really, you have no idea how sorry I am."

She smiled at him and said, "That's $28.60."

He paid his bill and gathered his bags. She looked at him and said, "I'll be here if you come back this way."

Jacob set down the bags he had in one hand, reached out and grabbed her right hand. He gently raised it to his lips and kissed it while looking her in the eyes.

"Thank you," he said softly. "You really made my day."

She looked at him, sighed and smiled, and said, "I'm looking forward to your return trip."

Jacob smiled back, picked up his bags and

walked out the door. Not once did he think about his headache or how sore he was from bushwhacking that nasty mountain. His mind was preoccupied with a pretty, little blond from the General Store. When he returned to the campsite, Diane almost had breakfast ready. She saw Jacob approach and asked, "What are you so glowing about?"

"Oh, nothing. I just had a nice conversation with the clerk in the store, that's all," he said.

"You're talking about that little blond, aren't you?" she asked smiling.

"Uh huh," he said. He smiled right back.

"Do we need to leave you here, man?" asked Parker laughing. "I've seen her, too. If I wasn't married…"

"Okay, stop right there," Diane yelled, "Before you get yourself in a rut you can't get out of."

Jacob laughed and said, "No, I don't need to stay. We need to move on as a team. We have ground to cover."

Diane looked at both men with a piercing look and said, "Breakfast is ready, wolves."

They all laughed and sat down, enjoying a great breakfast of eggs, bacon and some hot oatmeal. Shiloh was content eating his own food, but continually stared at Jacob looking for a handout. Jacob, however, learned his lesson about Shiloh and was not about to feed him anything for fear that the nuclear explosions from the dog's ass might start at any moment. When finished eating, they cleaned up, packed up their gear and headed for the Trail.

Chapter Eleven

The trio of hikers, and the dog, soon returned to the Trail and continued to head south. Parker mainly walked ahead, keeping an eye on Shiloh and his exploring every tree and bush, while Diane and Jacob eased back so they could talk.

"I know you were out there last night, sitting and waiting for Thomas to come back," she said. "I didn't feel his presence. He didn't come, did he?"

"No," replied Jacob with his head down. "I stayed out there till 4am, but it was noisy and I think he wanted more privacy."

Diane looked at him with a positive look and said, "You know he's coming back, don't you?"

"Yes," he said. "I really believe he will. And I hope he accepts you as my dear friend and realizes he can talk to both of us."

"Me, too, Jacob," she said. "Maybe the two of us together can figure out why he's here and find a way to release him."

"I just…feel so strongly that I can't leave this trip without finding his answer. I'll never be at rest knowing I couldn't help him if I left."

"I understand, Jacob," she said. "I think you'll go home satisfied."

Parker turned around and yelled back at the two, "You girls do more talking than walking. I told you she couldn't keep quiet."

"We two 'girls' have a lot to talk about," she yelled. "You just like walking with Shiloh because he doesn't speak."

"Bingo!" Parker yelled. "Jacob is giving me a break from having to strain my voice all day long with you. Thanks Jake!"

"It's Jacob," he yelled.

"I know. I'm fucking with ya, man," Parker exclaimed laughing.

Jacob looked at Diane with an inquisitive look and asked, "Is he always this annoying?"

"Yes," she said, "He is. But, you get used to it eventually."

"I don't have eventually," replied Jacob. "I only have now. He's annoying right now."

They looked at each other and laughed, knowing that Jacob was just joking around. He really liked Parker, in spite of all his quirks.

More hours passed with much more conversation taking place. Jacob was perfectly at ease with them there, knowing that Diane's goal was to help in any way she could. Both of them were hoping Thomas would arrive tonight and be at ease with the new friends that he recruited.

Just then, parker yelled out to them, "Hey, come here you guys! You gotta see this!"

They hurriedly ran up to where Parker and Shiloh were standing, staring up high in front of them. A large waterfall was flowing over the above rock face, creating a crystal, clear pool below with a misty spray everywhere.

"This looks like a great place to break for lunch and a swim," said Parker. Shiloh was already in the water swimming around, waiting for someone to throw a stick or join him in the water. Jacob found the piece of a small log and tossed it into the water. Shiloh almost caught it in mid-air before it hit with a huge splash. The crazy Labrador swam to it, picked it up and brought it back to Jacob.

"Now you did it," said Parker. "They're born retrievers. Once you start, he'll never stop. He'll drive you nuts."

"Hmmm...drive you nuts, huh," said Jacob. "I wonder where he gets that from."

Diane started laughing because she knew what Jacob was getting at, but Parker never caught on. He picked up the big stick and tossed in the water for Shiloh. "I'll save you from the hyper dog," he said. "Why don't you two ladies set up for lunch?"

"Sounds like a winner," said Jacob. He and Diane found a slab of rock to put out the spread of food. Diane insisted that Jacob save his food for farther down the Trail, when they finally separated and went their own ways. She made peanut butter and jelly sandwiches and had some small bags of chips for everyone. Parker joined them when he saw the food ready to eat. Plenty of water was available and they consumed quite a bit trying to wash down the peanut butter stuck in their mouths. After drinking their containers dry, they leaned over the rock and pumped more clean, filtered water into their bottles from the pool. It was an endless supply of cool, fresh water that they welcomed over and over. After lunch, they waded in the pool and rinsed their sweaty arms and faces with the misty spray from the high waterfall, cooling their skin and making them feel refreshed. A short time later, they were packed and back on the Trail.

Parker struck up a conversation while walking with Jacob. He asked, "So, Jacob, you're a Science Teacher, right?"

"That's correct," replied Jacob.

"Did you ever think about hosting a weekend camping trip with some of the students? You know, like a field trip?" asked Parker. "I bet you could show them a lot of things and they would learn so much."

Jacob pondered that thought a moment, and then replied,

"Well, I really never thought about doing that before. My mind has been pretty occupied with personal things over the years, so that really wasn't a possibility."

"What about now?" Diane asked. "This is supposed to be the trip that changes your life. Maybe after this trip is over, you can sit back and have time to think about what your future holds, and the future of your students."

Jacob knew that this could be a good idea, a way to bring students together and enhance their learning. Moreover, it would give them a chance to experience what's outside of their normal, routine home-life and get away from the TV's, cell phones and local hang-outs that they deal with every day. It really wasn't such a bad idea.

"I certainly couldn't do it alone, I'd need a lot of help with something like that," Jacob replied.

"Of course you would, man!" exclaimed Parker. "Even if you only had half-a-dozen or so students, it would be too much for one person to plan, set up things, supply and cook the food…that's why you have other teachers, parents and friends to help. Be like the armed forces…Recruit, man! Recruit!"

"Well, it's certainly something I'll think about when I get back," said Jacob. "It really is a great idea. Thanks."

"Absolutely, man," said Parker. "It's all about the kids, right? It's our job to make sure they get the best education we can give them."

For someone that was annoying as hell, Jacob thought, he really wasn't so bad after all. Being a counselor, he works with all types of kids and knows how they react to discipline and what their individual needs may be. This could even be something some of the more troubled kids needed, a way to get out of their everyday environment for a while and just mellow in the wilderness with new friends. There were plenty of places in Michigan to travel to, some great ones only a few hours away from the big city life, so there was no need to spend the entire day on the road to get to your destination. They would have the opportunity to learn about camping and hiking, survival and be surrounded by science and nature. This obviously wasn't for everyone, but the few that would attend a field trip like this would get the education of a lifetime, something they would never forget.

"You know, Jacob," Diane said, "This trip could have a lot more meaning than you think. It can have personal healing qualities for you, a great new future to open up for your students and a finality for Thomas."

"Thomas?" asked Parker. "That guy that told you about the cattails? How can this be a finality for *that* guy? Are you going to kill him for making you eat those raunchy things? That would be pretty final."

"We can't answer that right now, honey.

Hopefully you'll understand it sometime later on," Diane responded.

"Oh...WE can't answer that," replied Parker sarcastically. "Now WE have a secret to hide from Parker, do we?"

Jacob chimed in this time, "No secret, Parker. We just think you'll understand it better later on; when you see it firsthand. If it happens at all."

"And if it doesn't happen soon, we'll explain the whole thing to you when the time is appropriate," Diane said smiling.

"Deal," said Parker. "I suppose I can wait for a bit. I'm a sucker for surprises anyway."

A group of hikers approached them coming up the Trail, two men, one woman, four boys and two girls. The kids looked like high schoolers, maybe even early college. Shiloh went running towards them, jumping and wagging his tail. If a dog could smile, he would've been smiling at the sight of new friends to play with. Parker was the first to speak out, because that's just Parker.

"Hi guys! And gals!" he shouted.

"Hello," said one of the men. "That's a pretty friendly dog you have there."

"He is. But he'll tear your throat out if he doesn't like you," Parker said.

"Parker!" exclaimed Diane. "Don't listen to him. He thinks he's funny. And don't laugh at anything he says, it just fuels the fire."

Parker looked at the crowd with a smirk, shrugged his shoulders and chuckled.

"So, what do we have here," asked Jacob. "Family outing? School kids, maybe?"

The elder man, possibly in his mid-fifties, spoke up with an explanation.

"It's our annual hiking trip with some of the students from Elkton High School. Well, I say annual, but this really is only the second year. Last year's went so well, we decided to make it an annual outing."

Jacob, Diane and Parker all looked at each other, surprised.

"Man, is that ironic," Parker said. "We were just discussing the exact same thing before you popped up in front of us. Jacob, here, is a Science teacher back in Michigan, and I'm a Guidance Counselor from this area. My wife and I were telling him what a great thing it would be if he organized a hiking trip with some of his students."

"Ironic, you say?" asked the woman. She pointed to the older man and said, "Dave, here, is an English teacher that teaches his kids how to write essays. He has the kids keep daily journals to expand into stories later. Jeremy is our Shop teacher that loves to work with wood. He's very good at building rough shelters and improvising in the woods, especially teaching survival techniques. We call him Survivor man. I'm the Vice-Principal of the school. I come because I think the idea is great for the kids and I love the outdoors."

The young hikers stayed occupied playing with Shiloh, while the adults carried on with their conversation.

Jacob looked very interested in the whole concept, but was still skeptical about how to plan the trip.

"So, I'm sure something like this takes an incredible amount of time to plan and organize," Jacob said.

"I'll tell you what," said the Vice-Principal. "If you're really serious about doing something like this, I'll give you the person to talk to at our school. His name is Jeff and he's been our Activities Director for the past five years. He has plenty of ideas and can be a great asset to you when planning this out."

She reached in her shirt pocket, pulled out a small, spiral note pad, jotted down Jeff's name and number and handed it to Jacob.

"Thank you so much," Jacob said with a big smile.

"So glad to help," she said. "When we get back, I'll tell him you'll be contacting him."

"Thanks again...I'm sorry, what is your name?" he asked.

"Rose," she replied. "When you call him, tell him that Rose met you on the Trail and told you to call."

She turned toward the students and yelled, "C'mon kids! Say goodbye to the dog. We need to keep moving!"

Jacob reached out and shook hands with Rose, Dave and Jeremy.

"Thank you so much for this info and encouragement," he said. "I really think that this is something I can do."

"Of course you can," Rose said with excitement. "It's all about the kids, right?"

Jacob looked shocked, because those were the

exact words Parker used earlier when he brought up the idea. He looked at Parker and Diane; they were looking right at him, smiling. Parker had that smirk on his face as if he was saying, 'See? I know what I'm talking about.'

The kids came strolling back and they all bid their farewells, wishing safe travels to each other, continuing on their separate ways.

Evening was drawing near when Jacob recommended to the small group, "I think we better start looking for a shelter before it gets too late."

Diane reached into her side pocket and pulled out the Trail map. After finding their location, she said, "It looks like there might be one just about a mile ahead. Hopefully it's vacant and we can occupy it." She looked at Jacob and winked, both of them knowing that Thomas may be coming tonight.

They hiked on, the sun slowly sinking over the distant ridgeline, until they came upon a newly constructed, four-person shelter. It was empty.

"Woohoo!" exclaimed Parker. "No tent camping tonight!"

Like the other shelters similar in size, this one

also had a bunk bed at each side with a common table in the middle. There was plenty of room for all three, including Shiloh. In fact, Shiloh could even have his own lower bunk if he wanted. The wood framing and planked walls were newly built this year. It had a four-foot wide porch with an impressive overhang to shield from the rain, so cooking outside in bad weather was not a problem. The front design was the same as other shelters with a three-foot wood-framed wall on the lower half and screened window openings above. A standard wooden, screen door centered the wall.

The entire area was nestled inside a cluster of pines and spruce with a modest-sized clearing in front containing the fire pit. A small stream about two-feet wide, just past the trees flowed down the hillside to the valley floor, giving them access to plenty of water for drinking and cooking, but not before filtering. They all knew it wasn't advised to drink water straight from any source in the woods without filtering or purifying with iodine tablets, because the water contains too many micro-organisms and parasites that can make your life a living hell if ingested.

As before, when they sheltered together, Diane and Parker took the bunks on the right while Jacob moved in on the left. Parker took the top bunk, Diane the lower and Jacob set up his sleeping bag on the top, left bunk, leaving the lower open to Shiloh if he preferred. By this time, darkness settled in over the forest, so they unpacked some candle lanterns and lit them, placing them on the table and on the wood shelves inside. The soft touch of subdued light permeated the inside of the shelter, casting a romantic glow within. Diane and Parker sat at the table, softly talking to each other in a playful way. They snickered, looked into each other's eyes and held hands. Jacob glanced over occasionally and couldn't help but think of Annie and Jimmy. Annie was much like Diane, playful and romantic, but serious when she needed to be. She was the kind of woman that had it all together; she cherished life and its treasures. He often wondered why he was the lucky one to have had such a great partner as Annie. And that's what bothered him the most. He didn't *have* a great partner, he *had* a great partner. A great partner that gave birth to his great son, Jimmy. A cherished boy taken away from him way too soon. He couldn't help feeling sadness as he periodically glanced at the two at the table, but it also brought joy to his heart, knowing that this kind of love was shared by others. Jacob finally spoke up, "Hey, get a room you two."

Parker looked up and smiled, "This *is* our room," he said.

"That's what I was afraid of," said Jacob jokingly. "Just keep it down over there, please."

"Too late for that, man," Parker replied. "It's already up."

"Parker!" Diane screamed. "Stop torturing him!"

Jacob put his fingers in his ears, looked at the two and chanted aloud, "Lalalalala…lalalalala!"

They all started laughing hysterically, tightening the bond that they had for each other. Parker stood up, looked around the shelter and said, "I think it's time to rustle up some grub!"

"Who are *you* all of a sudden, John Wayne?" Diane asked.

"C'mon pretty lady, I gotta hankerin' for some cookin'," replied Parker.

"Okay Duke," Jacob said. "I'm with you."

They dug into their packs and pulled out their little camp stoves and food packs. The so-called kitchen they set up was out on the porch, away from the inside of the shelter. After all, Jacob knew first-hand what cooking inside a shelter could do. The hissing sound of the mini-burners were the only sound heard in the woods while Diane and Shiloh gathered firewood from nearby. Diane gathered armfuls of sticks and branches and Shiloh grabbed anything he could find, including small logs the size of your arm and six-feet long. Once there was enough wood to last through the night, Diane stacked the fire pit with some dry wood and pine needles, then lit the bundle. Before long, she had a great campfire blazing and tended the fire while the two men cooked.

The pots of water were beginning to bubble when Jacob zipped open a pouch with freeze-dried chicken and dumplings, while Parker prepared a dinner for two of dried noodles, broccoli and chicken. They both added the boiling water to the pouches of food and let them simmer for about ten minutes while boiling more water for coffee and tea. Parker set out a plastic bowl for Shiloh and filled it with dried dog food. They carried the completed entrees down to the fire where Diane was sitting and sat down, all content with their gourmet backpacking meals. Even Shiloh was happy.

The fire crackled while Diane and Parker sipped their hot coffee. Jacob had his tea, something he preferred over the strong coffee packets he bought earlier.

"Great job on the fire, honey," Parker said lovingly.

"Yes, indeed," chimed Jacob. "It always goes better when there's complete partnership and everyone chips in."

"Isn't that the way it should be?" asked Diane. "A partnership?"

"That's the way I look at it. And obviously, you guys, too," replied Jacob. "But there's a lot of couples out there that don't see it that way. You get those hardheaded, stubborn men that were raised believing the woman does all the work around the house and the man just brings home the money. That's a recipe for an unhappy marriage."

"And don't forget about the hardheaded, stubborn women," Parker noted.

"What's *that* supposed to mean?" asked Diane.

"Here we go," said Parker.

"No, really, what does that mean?" she asked again.

Jacob thought this was a good time to jump in to ease the tension. "He means that it's a two-way street, some women can be as stubborn as a man."

"Hold on, Jacob," Parker said. "Don't put words in my mouth and try to make it all cushy and everything. There's a true reality here."

"And what does THAT mean, SWEETHEART?" Diane said with an escalating voice.

"You know what it means. I'm talking about your mother."

Diane glared at Parker, not saying a word, but you could hear everything going on in her mind.

"Your mom wears the pants in the family," he said. "She always did. She controls your dad, controls what he does, controls what they do and when they do it, and controlled you and your sisters until it brought you to tears. YOU even told me that."

Diane, now realizing everything Parker said was true, nodded her head.

"You're right," she said softly. "You're both right. Women can be stubborn and controlling, too."

"High five, Jake!" exclaimed Parker, holding up his hand.

Jacob looked at Parker with a deadpan look, and then busted out laughing. He raised his hand to make contact with Parker's and said, "Okay, I guess because of this trip, my name is now Jake. You win."

"Bingo, baby!" he exclaimed. He stood up and walked towards the shelter.

"I'm going to unpack some stuff and get the sleeping bags ready. You two ladies can sit and talk."

Jacob looked over at Diane with a little smirk and said, "Just when you start to like him, he goes back to being annoying and you realize you're an idiot for even thinking he was okay."

Diane laughed. "Well, spend some time with him and you'll see he's really not so bad."

"I don't have that much time left in my life," Jacob said chuckling.

They both turned and stared into the fire for a moment, silent. Diane spoke first.

"Do you think Thomas will come tonight?" she asked quietly.

"I don't know," he said sorrowfully. "I hope he realizes that it's okay with you here and at least talks to *me*. I don't want to lose more time away from him and have him get discouraged and leave...forever."

"He'll come back, Jacob. He's not finished with you," she said. "He's looking for answers, and so are you. He will come back. Trust me."

"I hope you're right," he said looking down. Then he looked at her and said, "I do trust you. I really do."

She smiled and touched his hand to comfort his doubts. They sat, mostly in silence, and watched the fire crackle as they kept adding bigger logs to keep it burning into the night. At 10pm, they headed into the shelter for some sleep, hoping they would be awakened later by the presence of Thomas. Parker had fallen asleep on his upper bunk and Shiloh was on the floor, laying in front of the screen door keeping guard on not only the inside, but outside, too. The two of them quietly climbed into their respective bunks, bid each other a silent goodnight and hoped they would meet up with Thomas in a few hours.

Final Chapter

Shiloh perked up, looking outside the shelter screen door...tail wagging...not making a sound. It was 3:40am.

"He's here," Diane said softly.

Jacob raised his head and looked out at the campfire. The transparent figure of Thomas was approaching from the trees. Jacob quietly climbed down off his bunk and walked out the door to meet Thomas.

"I was worried I wouldn't see you again after last night. How are you, my friend?" asked Jacob.

"I'm...alright," answered Thomas. "I sense you're not alone, but I came anyway. I need answers, like you."

"You're right, I'm not alone, Thomas. The woman with me knows about you, but I didn't tell her husband yet. She's sincere and understanding and wants to help just as much as I do."

Thomas, trusting Jacob, nodded his head and agreed to let her come out to meet him.

Jacob motioned to the shelter for Diane to come out to the fire. She opened the screen door, keeping Shiloh inside and carefully stepped down off the porch. Parker was still asleep, but Shiloh watched silently through the screen door.

Diane approached slowly as to not startle Thomas and stood next to Jacob, staring in amazement at the misty figure standing before her of a worn down, tattered and beaten Confederate soldier in the form of a young, teenage boy.

"Diane, this is Thomas Garland Jefferson, grandson of President Thomas Jefferson," Jacob said softly. "Thomas, this is my good friend, Diane."

"Hello, Thomas," Diane said softly.

"Pleased to make your acquaintance, Miss Diane," said Thomas proudly.

Parker awoke at the sound of voices outside. He looked around and saw nobody was in the shelter except the dog, then climbed off his bunk and stood there with Shiloh, staring through the screen door.

Parker saw Diane and Jacob at the fire, talking with a misty figure of a...Confederate soldier? He was definitely confused and couldn't believe what he was seeing. Shiloh believed it was someone, but Parker wasn't sure what he was looking at.

"Thomas, I've told Diane everything that we've talked about...that I believe you're still here wandering because there's unfinished business left for you to do," Jacob said with a heartwarming voice. "Diane has the ability to sense spirits. She knew you were at the other shelter when she and her husband were with me and you left. She also just said at 3:40...'he's here'. She can feel your presence."

Diane asked, "Are you okay with us being here, Thomas?"

Thomas looked around for a moment and replied, "Yes ma'am. I have a good feeling about it."

"That's good, Thomas. We don't want you to be upset or uncomfortable," Jacob said.

They all sat down around the campfire to talk, Jacob tossing on another couple of logs to keep it going for a while. Thomas was encouraged to tell his story to Diane, which he did proudly and with ease.

After conversing back and forth with questions

and answers, Diane asked, "Thomas, do you have any idea at all why you've been drawn to Jacob on his hike through this trail? Have you been drawn to anyone before?"

"No one before, ma'am," Thomas replied. "I've had other souls walk with me, but I've never really searched out for anyone until he came along. It seems that this started to happen when the little boy showed up."

"Little boy?" asked Diane.

"Thomas told me a while ago that there was a little boy that walked with him sometimes," Jacob clarified.

"Oh, that's right, and who do you think this little boy is, Thomas?" Diane asked.

"I don't know. He just started showing up," Thomas said. "He first appeared right before I met Jacob."

Suddenly, Diane started feeling something. She had a strong feeling they were being watched and wasn't quite sure what was going on. But she knew it was some kind of spirit nearby. She perked up and looked around into the trees.

"What is it?" asked Jacob.

"I'm not sure, I feel something…someone."

Jacob asked, "Are we in danger?"

"No," said Thomas. "Do not fear."

Diane stood up, motionless, looking around. "He's here, too."

"Who's here?" asked Jacob.

"The little boy. He's here."

Diane and Jacob looked around the campsite waiting to see what was to appear. Thomas pointed across the clearing into the trees and said, "There."

A short, misty figure stepped out of the trees and started to materialize. It was a young boy with blond hair. Jacob looked…stared…shook his head in disbelief… "I think…oh my God…it can't be…I think it's…Jimmy."

"Your son, Jimmy?" Diane asked shockingly.

"Yes," Jacob replied choking up.

As the figure became clearer, there was no doubt that it was Jimmy, Jacob's son. Jacob dropped to his knees, his emotions overtook him, and he couldn't believe his eyes. "Diane…my God…do you see him?" Jacob mumbled.

"Yes, Jacob…I see him," she said. Tears were starting to flow from her eyes, too. Parker still watched from the shelter in amazement at what was happening. He had always been a skeptic to these things and couldn't believe it was happening right in front of him.

Jimmy, nearly a solid figure now, walked towards Jacob. He stopped a few feet in front of him. Diane and Thomas looked on. Jacob could barely see what was going on because of his tears.

"It wasn't your fault, dad," Jimmy said softly.

Jacob broke down into a sob. He covered his face and cried uncontrollably.

"You need to stop blaming yourself for something that wasn't your fault. You couldn't have done anything about it," Jimmy said lovingly.

Jacob looked up, still crying and said to Jimmy, "But if I was there with you and mom it may have turned out different."

"No dad, it wouldn't have," Jimmy said. "This is the way it was supposed to be. I'm sorry, too."

Something suddenly clicked in Diane's head. A realization. "Jacob...this is it!" she said excitedly, but softly.

Jacob looked over to her and said, "I don't understand. This is what?"

"This is why Thomas has been wandering

around following you. Don't you see?" she exclaimed. "It was his final mission to bring Jimmy to you so he could tell you himself that it wasn't your fault, to stop blaming yourself after eight, painful years and get on with the rest of your life. This is it! This is the whole reason you're here!"

Jacob looked as though he suddenly had a weight lifted. It all made sense. This backpacking trip after eight years of guilt was for him to clear his head and get a grip on his life, somehow. A trip into the Civil War battle areas brought a lost, wandering Confederate soldier to him that didn't know why he wasn't at peace or why he was following Jacob, but he was. A little boy recently appeared with the soldier before Jacob showed up on the Trail and Thomas didn't know why he was there. Jacob now realized it has come full circle.

"I think I get it now. Thomas' mission was to bring my son to me, for one last moment. To tell me not to feel guilty for something that I had no control over and live my life the way it was intended, happy and guilt-free," said Jacob.

Diane leaned down and hugged Jacob while both of them cried.

"You see Jacob," she said. "People come into your life for a reason."

"And that's why you and Parker came into mine…to help me look deep into my soul, realize what all this meant and bring me to this moment."

Jacob looked back at Jimmy, smiling between the tears.

"I didn't know when I said goodbye to you and mom that night that it was going to be the last time I saw you both," Jacob said sadly. He looked into Jimmy's eyes, "I wish there was a way I could just hug you one more time, son."

Jimmy paused…looked up into the dark sky for a moment, as if to get approval, then nodded and looked back into Jacob's teary eyes. He then began materializing from a misty, semi-transparent figure into a completely solid one until he looked like a normal human being, standing within arm's length of his dad. He stretched out his arms, walked to his dad and threw his arms around him. Jacob wrapped his arms tightly around his son one last time.

"I love you, daddy," whispered Jimmy into Jacob's ear.

Jacob could barely get out the words, "I love you

too, Jimmy."

After a few moments, they released each other and Jimmy stepped back, looked at Thomas and took his hand. They turned and walked across the clearing together. A blinding ray of dense, misty, bright light suddenly appeared and beamed down from high above the trees, shining onto a spot on the other side of the clearing.

Jimmy and Thomas stepped into the light, turned and faced Jacob and Diane.

Jimmy looked up at Thomas and said, "It's time to go, Thomas. It's time to go home."

Jacob looked at them both. Thomas spoke first.

"Thank you, Jacob," he said. "I can go home now."

"No...thank YOU Thomas," said Jacob chokingly. He looked at his son and said, "Thank you, my son. You've changed me forever."

"It was time, dad. It was finally time," said Jimmy lovingly. "I love you, daddy."

Jacob stood to his feet, legs wobbly. With tears in his eyes, he spoke softly and said, "Goodbye, Jimmy. I love you too."

Jimmy looked directly into his dad's eyes and

said, "It's not goodbye, dad…it's I'll see you later."

Jimmy and Thomas, hand in hand, looked at each other and nodded. Seconds later, they…and the light…were gone.

The screen door opened and Parker came outside, Shiloh right behind. "What the…." expressed Parker.

Diane and Jacob stood staring at each other, smiling with tears. She took his hand and they walked towards the shelter.

Parker stood watching with his mouth open and said, "What…did I just…wait…I'm confused."

"How do you feel, Jacob?" Diane asked quietly.

Jacob tried to speak, but was only able to mumble the words, "I don't even know what to say."

As they walked past Parker, Parker kept staring at the clearing where the bright light had been, consuming Jimmy and Thomas. He walked over to it and tried to examine the area, but of course found nothing. Shiloh sniffed around; excitedly wagging his tail knowing something was there previously, but also found nothing.

"I feel…like…a new man," Jacob said surprisingly. "I now know they're safe and I *will* see them again. We'll be together as a family like we used to be."

Diane smiled looking at him. "They want you to live a full, productive life, Jacob. That means being the teacher you're used to being, doing the crazy things for your students that not only keep them interested, but helping them learn great things about Science. And who knows, maybe organizing and attending fantastic hiking trips for those special students that need that special attention."

Words of wisdom spoken by a truly sincere woman with exploding compassion. He knew she was right. He was the one that understood what his students needed to keep their attention. He was the one they looked up to for learning and the reason for coming back to school every day. He was the one that could make a difference in their life and their future. He...was Mr. Wizard.

Just before the new school year started, Jacob had a meeting with the School Board and with their unanimous approval and help; he created "The Allen Memorial Fund", in honor of Annie and Jimmy. This charity accepted donations that were dedicated to make it possible for students to attend Jacob's annual camping and hiking weekend, taking up to a dozen students on a weekend trip into the northern woods of Michigan. Of course, more than one adult needed to come along to help with, well, everything. Preferably, someone that knew something about backpacking and the wilderness. Jacob had no trouble finding a couple of people that were willing to help him manifest this opportunity for the kids.

Diane and Parker were honored and excited to make the trip to Michigan every year, not only to help with the students, but to continue and strengthen that special bond they were so fortunate to create along that great stretch of the Appalachian Trail in Shenandoah National Park. Shiloh was also part of the mix, keeping the students busy throwing sticks and licking everyone around the campfires. The kids learned about the qualities of life outside of the city, camping and hiking techniques, the art of survival in an emergency, Science, and, thanks to Thomas, the delicious taste of cattails as an emergency food source. Of course, Diane told the kids to make sure you cut off the lower part of the stem before eating, and it was ritual for them to tell the students about Jacob's experience with the delectable, nutritious, muck tasting vile weed. That always got a good laugh around the campfire. The popular, annual outing became known as "Wizards of the Woods," the name being dubbed by the students themselves in honor of Mr. Wizard.

After years of needless suffering from his own guilt trip, Jacob Allen, Mr. Wizard to his students, could not be a happier man.

About the Author

James Allen Trick, affectionately known as Jimmy, has had a love for writing since Junior High School when he was assigned to write an essay on any subject. Turns out, he had the knack and was one of four students chosen out of 100 to enter the advanced writing class.

Throughout his life, he continued writing by journaling his backpacking adventures, turning them into short stories. Due to some unique and unexpected events, it seemed that each trip became a humorous tale.

His first love is his family, but Jimmy is a multi-layered man. In no particular order, here are the other "loves of his life": adventure, the great outdoors, motorcycle riding, skydiving, Civil War history enthusiast and the world of the paranormal.

Combining his interest in the Civil War, his love for the outdoors and the intrigue of ghostly phenomenon is what prompted him to write **GUILT TRIP**, a fictional adventurous story about spirits and the afterlife.

In 2007, Jimmy decided to expand his interest in things-that-go-bump-in-the-night by becoming a Certified Paranormal Investigator. He founded **Goosebumps Paranormal Society**...*a* ghostly group of investigators that examines anything and everything eerie, spooky, or bizarre. Their slogan is, "Contact US, when they contact YOU!". The group and their investigating skills were featured on Animal Planet's ***'Finding Bigfoot'***.

Follow them on their Facebook page:

GOOSEBUMPS PARANORMAL SOCIETY

Check out their informative website at:

www.goosebumpsparanormalsociety.weebly.com

Made in the USA
Columbia, SC
20 August 2017